pigiron

pigiron

DAVID JAMES KEATON

BURNT BRIDGE || NEW ORLEANS || MINNEAPOLIS

Pig Iron is a work of fiction. Names, characters, places, and incidents are the products of the author's imagination or are used fictitiously. Any resemblance to actual events, locales, or persons, living or dead, is entirely coincidental.

Portions of this novel previously appeared as short stories in the following publications:
"Three Ways Without Water (or The Day Roadkill, Drunk Driving, and the Electric Chair Were Invented)" in *Pulp Modern II*, "Ha'penny Dreadfuller" in *Burrow Press Review*, and "Smelt (or A Gun Named Sioux)" in *The Big Adios*.

http://burntbridge.net

Cover art by Tony McMillen
Cover design by Dyer Wilk
Cover design concept by Jason Stuart
Interior design by Mark Rapacz
Interior art by Ben Wetherbee

LIBRARY OF CONGRESS CATALOGING-IN-PUBLICATION DATA

ISBN-13: 978-1-941601-03-7
ISBN-10: 1941601030

For my dad, who first played me the Marty Robbins song "Big Iron," right before we both tried to turn it into a movie. Thanks for working on this with me, and thanks for all those westerns.

TABLE OF CONTENTS

PROLOGUE

Ha'penny Dreadfuller

"It's just that I think my heart and soul are kind of famished. I'm sorry, sorry, sorry, sorry, I'm sitting feeling sorry in the Thirsty Dog."
-Nick Cave, "Thirsty Dog"

Agua Fría, New Mexico, 9:09 a.m. Spring of 1878.

The coyote stopped at the edge of the well, a warning rumbling in her throat. On the way up the hill, her entire body telegraphed a change in the air. The smell of decay pulsed in her nostrils, and her tail was working overtime, whiplashing the flies from the furless patches of skin of her haunch. The signals ran from one end of her body to the other. Heat begat the smell, begat the flies, begat the tail. She was used to such stimuli and response hardwired into her frantic gait, even without the all-consuming hunger that increasingly clouded her mind. At the rim of the stone circle, however, she found no evidence of water or the potentially nourishing rot her senses were screaming for. She leaned out to nose the rope creaking down in the darkness. The weight of a bucket hung suspended from it, now swaying over an empty hole, where it had previously bobbed and sloshed years before. Her snout nudged the rope to swinging, but the weight of the gold coins heaped inside slowed and stopped it pretty quick.

Before the well had dried up, when the bucket had still been half underwater, the waves of sunlight playing against these coins had kept most every horsefly at bay. Now the bucket hung limp and splintered, baking in the daylight and this new brick oven, and the gold coins had lost the dance of their former amplified reflection. The coyote didn't know a dance of light was an amazing natural deterrent to any insect. To her, everything was just a new source of agony.

And now, without the shine of the water, the flies could bite and sting her sores with impunity.

But she was ready to make the trade, winged torment for the promise of carrion. And although the coyote had no way of knowing this booty was the cause of today's misery, or at least these riches were no longer working with the shimmering well water to make her world more bearable, she had experienced a reprieve once before.

A week earlier, she'd swallowed a penny while lapping water from a teacup, one of fifty balanced along a rancher's fence posts. This rancher had left cups of water and copper along his border in order to keep his daughter from being troubled by flies at her upcoming nuptials. But the rancher had caught the coyote upending the cup, and had even taken a shot at her, despite her daughter's pleas to please, please leave her be, as the rancher's daughter had seen the low hang of the coyote's belly that concealed an imminent birth. This was a condition the rancher's daughter knew something about, also the reason her wedding was being held in a dusty backyard rather than a nearby church, or even the rancher's gun store, where his own brother had tied the knot two years before. But her wedding would never occur, not because of the swarms, but because the groom never showed. However, the rancher's daughter's belly wouldn't wait for another suitor.

The three of them would eventually gather the rest of the pennies in silence, the baby in her belly kicking against the jostle of her sobs.

The pups inside the coyote kicked against dream space as their mother nosed the rope again, hoping for any last splash of moisture or mud to chew. But due to increasing desperation, but mostly due to the change in her center of gravity, she leaned too far over the edge of the well, and she tumbled on in.

The flies followed her down at their leisure.

Years later, the rancher would leave his dying crops behind and drag a cot into his bankrupt gun store, first uprooting his daughter and his strange little grandson, then kicking them out of his life in disgrace. And this bucket of gold would go undiscovered for a decade, until drought turned every well in the state into a treasure hunt. The celebration of a local gang who would one day discover these riches would be muted due to drunkenness and dehydration, but the leader of the gang would be excited enough to lean over the rim when he caught a flash of gold on the bottom. Not realizing this was a copper Indian headdress circa 1893 rather than Lady Liberty's profile that shined in the rib cage of the coyote's ghostly outline, and not far from the skulls of her litter, his greed would send him crashing to the bottom after it.

His gang would leave him down there for a long, long time, punishing him for grudges real and imagined, but mostly leaving him down there due to forgetfulness as they divided up the gold on booze and debts, fully expecting him to be dead when they returned, ready to pretend his death was a surprise.

But the leader of the gang had been underestimated since birth, weakness assigned by strangers due to pale skin prone to sunburn and blazing orange hair. He would survive his long nights in the well by counting the tiny skulls in the cradle of bones and sucking on that penny, fooling his body with the extra saliva that this created. He would survive months down there through pure force of will, amazed to find the well provided everything he needed. And every night would be a lesson in resentment, something he'd remember for the rest of the life. And although there were about a dozen other lessons he learned at the bottom of that well, like lessons in resilience, stubbornness, and determination, he would focus only on recitations that fortified him with hatred, the surprise secret of immortality, as he sucked on a penny and talked to his dogs.

ONE

The First Hole

"He was vicious and a killer, though a youth of twenty-four.
And the notches on his pistol numbered one and nineteen more."
-Marty Robbins, "Big Iron"

Agua Fría, New Mexico, 12:03 p.m. Summer of 1895.

Out of the shadows of an inconspicuous, half-buried, thousand-year-old meteorite comes a man on a horse with a ray of sunlight shining through a hole in its head. This hole, directly between the horse's ears and eye sockets, just below the crest of its cranium and just above the hinge of its mandible, runs completely through the skull, and, impossibly, when this horse shakes its head to snort the dust from its septum, the last flashes of the day flicker on and off one end of the tunnel like Morse code from a madman. The man atop his impossible horse is hard to see, just a black silhouette swimming in the limbo between the shade of the meteor and the glare of the sinking sunset behind him. He slowly leads the animal toward a group of five more cowboys lined up along a sagging wooden gate. Their hats are down over their eyes and faces, and combined with the mud covering identical workmanlike attire, this makes them utterly interchangeable. Only their voices finally distinguish them from one another, except maybe the first cowboy in the line, whose tone of bemused defeat sounds as weary as everyone else left in their world, but still seasoned with a bit of mirth. Laughing, this first cowboy steps forward to grab the bridle of the horse with the hole in its head.

"Damn," he says. "You have got to be the first man in history to ride a dead horse."

The shadow on the horse says nothing, and a second cowboy slides off the busted worm fence to walk up with his buddy. He puts a hand under the horse's nostrils. The beast is pale white, with a diseased glaze of red and yellow around its vacant eyes, ribs easily visible through its hide. Its legs are all bone and bad angles, and even the flies buzzing around the ass end seem confused when the horse's tail doesn't even bother to chase them away. A third cowboy gets up off the ground where the gate posts disappear into the dirt, pulling his hat further down over his eyes as he steps up. A fourth cowboy shuffles behind him, fear twitching in corners of his eyes.

"It ain't dead…" Second cowboy says to the Third. "…then it's probably just addle-headed and still breathin'."

Third cowboy starts to put a finger in the hole in the horse's head, then stops. He grips its jawbone under a sagging ear, and turns its snout towards him instead.

"Naw, it's dead," says First Cowboy again. "There ain't no heartbeat."

"There ain't no heart in its head, stupid," Second Cowboy frowns.

"I know where its heart is," Third Cowboy argues. "*This* is where you're supposed to grab a horse to feel its heart."

"Says who?"

"Someone smarter than your mouth, so don't argufy… but to be truthful, I presently don't remember."

"You're telling me that one time you came across another walkin', talkin' horse with a hole in its head, and on that day, someone told you it was still alive, proving this fact by pickin' its ear?"

"No, this is the first one I've ever seen, but..."

"But nothin'. It ain't dead. The bullet just drilled out some memories, that's all. And if it could talk, maybe it wouldn't be able to tell you about its first pair of shoes, I'll grant you that, but that's all it would have forgotten."

"Or tell you the location of the last place it dropped a shit."

"Can you?"

"Can who what?"

"Remember the last place you shit."

"Yeah. Thursday. In yer last pair of shoes."

A smallish fifth cowboy leaning on the fence barks loud at this, and the others jump.

"Fuck!" Third Cowboy bleats. "Forgot you were here. On Earth."

They all laugh, then trail off nervously, looking to the dark silhouette high on the impossible horse. This rider is still just an eclipse, the sun a red halo behind his body, leather glove creaking on the saddle horn. Third Cowboy releases the horse's head and walks around the animal to confront the rider.

"Don't drop the 'apple'!" he taunts the rider. Then, "Why *did* you buy that dead bay anyway?"

The rider says nothing as he reaches down to stroke the horse's head. All the cowboys step back and groan in disgust when the rider's hand runs affectionately over the hole in its skull, absently dipping in a finger like it's nothing.

"So, you finally bought it, we can see that," Third Cowboy smirks up at the shadow, nervous as always. "I gotta say though, interesting way to drive down the price."

"Why the hell would he want a dead horse?" Fifth Cowboy scoffs, defiant. "Even if it ain't dead, which it *is*, it ain't strong, it ain't fast, it ain't..."

"I reckon the man on this horse is fast enough for both of them," Second Cowboy says.

"Hold on. I thought that man who owned that horse *swore* he'd never sell it to no one, not for no amount of ballast. Especially our man Red here."

"I'm guessin' by the silence around these parts that no one sold no one nothin'."

"I'm guessin' you might be right. Let's ask the auger!"

The rider turns the horse away from Third Cowboy and backs it up a couple steps. Someone laughs and suddenly drops to start clawing at the dirt, looking for a mysterious something or other.

"Listen, boys," he says from the ground. "I'll bet you a bottle I can throw a rock clean through that horse's head."

Second Cowboy on the broken fence line jumps down from his post and stands up straight and tall, suddenly interested in the scene. The rider backs his horse up another step and his hand stops stroking its head and drifts toward the gun on his hip. Fifth Cowboy doesn't see this and keeps on talking.

"Why the fuck you buying dead horses, boss?" Fifth Cowboy says, laughing louder. "Wait! I know why! Because it's the only thing you ever shot that didn't die?"

"Naw, just always had something about holes."

This riddle makes everyone take a collective step backwards. They're a little older and have a better memory of the rider and the hole he means. Scratching his face with a shaky hand, Fifth Cowboy glances around, realizing he may have said too much. The shadow on the impossible horse is still blocking the sun, but now completely motionless except for a hand hovering over his gun, his first two fingers casually walking in the air above the trigger. Fifth Cowboy holds up both palms, the universal signal of an apology, even during dark days like these.

"Whoa, whoa, didn't mean nothing calling your new bangtail dead 'n' all."

The rider finally flicks his hat up off his eyes, and flies scatter, then light back on the sides of his face, looking for sweat. One scurries under a curl of red hair over his ear, and the rider doesn't even scratch, flies as familiar to him as the wind. When he speaks again, his voice is high, always surprisingly young and amused to anyone not used to his way.

"No, you're right. It *is* dead. And just like you and me, it don't know it yet."

TWO

Nefarious Chicken Wire Deceptions

"The beast in me is caged by frail and fragile bonds.
Restless by day and by night, rants and rages at the stars."
-Nick Lowe, "The Beast In Me"

Doña Ana, New Mexico, 12:03 p.m.

The Ranger Bob Ford is sitting in the dirt behind his farmhouse, looking down at the twisted wire of a chicken cage. The sides of the mangled cage are speckled with an explosion of blood and feathers. He squints in anger and disbelief at his skid marks in the ground, indulging in a bit of nostalgia while a rusted gun rests on his knee. He's motionless, the sun sinking in the distance, a rolled-up stack of posters on the ground by his boots. The visage of one particular poster has been stomped and kicked around, and through the mud stains only the word "Wanted!" is visible. A large raccoon peeks out from the warped wooden porch steps, and the Ranger levels his filthy revolver to kill it. The raccoon runs for the chicken innards, a streak of black and gray barely adjusts its beeline for the bloody cage even when he cocks the hammer, and the Ranger laughs, wondering how the animal knows it has nothing to fear from his weapon.

***

Agua Fría, New Mexico, 12:03 p.m.

"I seen the Preacher today, Mama."

"That's not the Preacher. Someone stole the Preacher's coat, I told you."

"But how do you know?"

"Because that tub-thumper left town when the water did."

"But we still have water, Mama."

McKenna Wendler grabs her son's arm high, near the shoulder, almost lifting him up off the ground.

"Listen to me now, Robby. You don't ever say that to anyone, you hear me? We don't have any water either. No one has water. And if you think of it, you ask anyone you see for water. We're dying, remember?"

"I'm sorry, Mama. We're dying. I'll try to remember."

"That's a good boy."

"Mama, have you seen the horse?"

"Whose horse," she asks, with that stiff lack of inquisitiveness that Robby recognizes as meaning his mother knows blame well whose horse.

"The horse with the hole in its head."

McKenna stares at her son, horrified by this detail. She expects his eyes to hold her worry, but instead they're bright and curious.

"It's okay, Mama. It has a hole in its head, but it doesn't care."

"What does that tell you?" she asks, hoping for an answer that makes some sense.

"It tells me it beat the Dutch! It tells me a hole in your head ain't that bad after all."

McKenna closes her eyes, no idea what to say to anything these days.

***

Later that day. The shadow rider atop the impossible horse with the hole in its head sits frozen, a hand over his holster, towering over four men standing in a loose circle around him. He's still blocking a sunset that seems reluctant to disappear into their airish evening red. Then someone belches and the sun is finally down, and the rider is out of all shadows, face brighter now than during any hour of the day, hat tipped back to show blazing eyes and rust-colored hair.

"I've been thinking, boys," Red says. "How many horses have I stolen?"

Al Mutters, a.k.a. "Mud," stands on one side of Red's horse, and Little Joe hides behind the other. Ned Parker, a particularly skeletal man they all call "Egg," stands near the sagging worm fence, his filthy legs blending in with the weary, wizened structure. Jack Hicks, a.k.a. "Jackass," kicks at the dirt near a post hole like it's the most important thing in the world. All the while, a fifth cowboy still has his hands high up in front of him, fear making his cracked fingertips shiver.

No one talks awhile, and soon all the scrawny, dust-covered men are straight and still, waiting to see what Red is going to do. Dread hangs in the air between them, the expectation that comes from seeing Red do many horrible things of late. Heads creak lower than normal on their aching necks, every face dark and hidden under the shade of their hats.

"At least 50," Fifth Cowboy sighs. He's the newest member of the gang, still missing a nickname, even missing a real name. Little Joe leans around the ass of the horse, mouth open to ask who the hell he was, and Mud points at him to shut up.

"And how old am I?" Red asks everyone.

"23," Fifth Cowboy answers.

"And how many women has this here biggity bub fucked in this town?"

"All of them."

"How many's that?"

"At least 30? Back when there was 30."

"And how old am I again?"

"Still 23, boss."

"And how many men I killed?"

Red holds a hand up before the man can answer. Instead he cocks a thumb back at Little Joe.

"I don't know, boss," Little Joe says. "I ain't been around you long enough, but I've seen you kill at least 10."

"He's killed 20," Mud says, blinking slow, mumbling. "No blusteration."

Mud sports a long, droopy mustache, and sometimes his voice is buried behind it.

"And how old am I again?"

"Still 23, boss," Mud says.

"And what's wrong with those numbers?" Red laughs.

Nobody says anything. One of them starts muttering Bible verse to fill the silence.

"*It's hard for thee to kick against the pricks…*"

"I was doing some thinking, boys," Red says. "And I was thinking that a man should have stole as many horses, fucked as many women, and killed as many men as the number of years he's been on this Earth. That means this can be the last horse I'll steal for a while, your sisters can be the last I've nailed to the counter for a while… but I'll be needing to catch up on that other number. Hell, I figure if I'm at least within three, I'll be satisfied."

"Why within three?" Fifth Cowboy asks, hands still up, palms out, legs together, but knees bent and ready to step back. Red studies him, smiling, noting the man's head isn't tilted ever so gently to the side, like his own.

"I don't know! Seems like good number, with the Father, the Son, and the Holy Spirit and all that shit. Within three, and I won't have an unhealthy obsession with numbers and bed men down for no good reason."

Red rolls his neck to crack it a bit. Bones pop like kindling.

"And then there's the fact we've all got three days to live," he shrugs. "That bad medicine hangs over my head a bit."

The men all kick dust and shuffle their feet, nervous. Egg is chewing on his lip like it's tobacco. Someone is still quoting Acts 9: 5-6.

"*What wilt thou have me do…*"

"Well, boss," Fifth Cowboy says, coughing. "If you're 23 years old, you're within that 'three' right now..."

But now this man has switched from staring down the nostril

of a dead horse to staring down the barrel of a gun. Red drew so fast no one saw nor heard the action. And everyone is suddenly scratching their dusty heads, like Little Joe desperate to remember this man's name, just in case they ever get a chance to tell the story later in life. They won't.

"You're right, boy," Red says. "Only today is my birthday."

The handle of Red's revolver squeaks under his squeeze, and his finger curls around the trigger like the tail of a whipped dog. The trigger tilts the seesaw of the strut, and the hammer is loosed to fly for the bulls-eye stamped on the base of the cartridge.

When men are dying of thirst, simple actions like this seem to take forever and become conducive to memorization, but in spite of the apparent complications of the gunshot, no one remembers the man's name nor the nature of his demise before or after the bullet's journey.

***

Doña Ana, New Mexico, 12:04 p.m.

Arizona Ranger Bob Ford's rusted revolver explodes in his fist, showering his face and shoulders with hot shrapnel from the burst barrel and the warm drizzle of his own blood.

"Jesus Christ!"

The Ranger stumbles back and sits in the dirt, watching the raccoon blink at him in confusion then turn and run off with a red fistful of chicken. A man steps from the trees behind the Ranger and stands staring at the Ranger's back for a moment. Then he walks around the Ranger and speaks. It's Tom McMaster, a young man in his 20s, one of the cowhands Bob flagged as eager for a law-enforcement father figure. The Ranger has always hated the genus.

"Got a letter for you, Ranger," Tom says, then sniggers as he watches the Ranger pull his sleeve up over his wounded hand. "You know something? While I walked up, I pulled my gun and put it back in the holster six times, and you never flinched."

The Ranger doesn't turn around. Instead, he just reaches behind his back with his good hand and holds it open. Tom slaps the letter into the stigmata of his palm.

"No way you're beef-headed enough to pull on me," the Ranger says. "So why lie about it?"

"You swearing us in tomorrow?"

"Everybody but you, Tom. Unless you quit asking."

Tom steps back to let the Ranger read his letter, shaking his head as he watches him get blood all over it.

***

Agua Fría. Dusk.

A young Mexican woman breastfeeds her baby in an adobe house packed with starving, howling cats. Outside the gaping doorway, in the dying, lingering light of the day, Red rides up to the porch and dismounts his horse with the hole in its head. He walks through the door, throwing his crushed hat against the wall in an explosion of dust, stripping a few rust-colored hairs from his scalp along with it. Red is a younger man when he stands in the shadows, strawberry blonde the last time he bathed, with a surprisingly innocent face around his wild eyes, anger, and dehydration. He has flecks of blood along one cheek outlining the half laugh he holds onto as he walks toward the woman and her baby. He dangles a tangle of chicken wire from his coat sleeve, then throws it at them as she shields the child.

"Your chickens are dead, dummy. Use this on the windows to keep out the cats." He points at the baby. "Pretty soon those noisy animals are gonna stop asking for food and start takin'…"

He wades through the desperate felines, kicking animals and wire out of his way, stomping up to stand in front of the cowering woman. One boot comes down heavy on the tail of a huge, ratty tom. It screeches and howls, and the rest of the cats scatter out the door. Red doesn't blink, not even when the tomcat, still pinned, twists around his boot, biting and clawing at the leather, its back legs rabbit-kicking Red's leg in vain. Red takes no notice of this at all, and his smile grows.

"Put that sucker away. It's my turn on that thing!"

The woman stares in horror at Red's boot heel still grinding the cat's tail, then quickly moves to lay the baby in its box. She tries in vain to release the child, but it hangs on to her breast by its teeth, stretching the woman like taffy. The cat's howls are deafening, and combined with the baby spitting milk down the woman's stomach and shrieking along with it, the woman fights the urge to crack her own skull against the dirt floor in despair. The cat bites hard into his boot, eyes crazed, and the woman relaxes a bit, imagining her own teeth sinking into Red's leather. Red just crosses his arms, still oblivious to the discord and palpable desperation hanging in the dust. He nods at the white bubbles burbling between the baby and her tortured nipple.

"Come on, no kid needs that much to drink. I know you like spices, but you beaneaters have to conserve like the rest of the town."

"With baby it's not '*drink*,'" she says in broken English. "It's '*eat*.'"

"You heard me. Hurry up before you yean another. Now where's my teat?"

With one hand, the woman hands him a bottle of whiskey, and he laughs and swigs half the alcohol almost instantly. With her other hand, she finally frees the baby from her body with an audible *Pop!* and shakes the dirt off a blanket to tuck around its shoulders. The cat, still trapped but not giving up, strains to climb Red high enough to lock on the bit of bare leg where his jeans shredded just above his boot. The cat stretches up and up and snaps into his calf, ears back and snarling so low the woman feels the triumph in her chest. Rivers of blood stain his leg like lightning at dusk, but Red just blinks a little slower. Seeming to notice the cat for the first time, he puts his full weight on its tail, and it howls so high it's inaudible for a good few seconds. Then Red coughs down the last drops of whiskey, absentmindedly throwing the half-empty bottle against the wall. It ricochets and lands inside the wooden box makeshift crib, shattering over the infant's face. The baby wails so loud that the cat stops working Red's leg and tries to climb into his boot and hide. Horrified, the woman runs to her baby, hands shaking as she pulls whiskey-soaked shards from its hair. Red turns to leave, disgusted.

"Too goddamn noisy in here. Your *mamacita* been blacksmithing you again?"

"What you do?" the Mexican woman cries.

"Relax. That kid ain't had nothing but rocks for toys since it's been born. It's gonna *need* that drink."

"Go!"

Red kicks the cat through the open window, then tosses a pewter hip flask onto the floor near the woman as an afterthought as he walks out. She comforts the injured child as best she can, trying to lick her fingers to help clean the cuts. After a moment of staring down the flask on the dirt floor, her mouth too dry to produce saliva and her body too dry to produce more milk, she eventually retrieves it from the floor and unscrews the top to take a deep drink of whiskey. Then, sobbing in silence, she leans down to wrap the chicken wire around the baby's wooden box, the hexagons casting shadows like honeycomb over the pinched, pink face. This lullaby of creaking metal calms them both a bit, and, no longer weeping, she finally presses the metal lip of the flask to the baby's eager mouth.

THREE

A Month of Guns and Sundays

"Stagger Lee shot Billy. Oh, he shot that poor boy so bad that the bullet went through Billy, and it broke the bartender's glass."
-Wilson Pickett, "Stagger Lee"

Bisbée, Arizona. Summer of 1853.

Little Bobby Ford, long before he rode south to become a big Texas Ranger, is aiming a finger at a hill in the distance while his father, Samuel, looks on. Bobby's dad is a big man with a sunburned face that masks his age. He is struggling to put a large revolver in his son's hands. Although Bobby will be a feared lawman one day, for now his hands are so small that he can only reach the trigger with the tip of his middle finger.

His father knows this is no way to hold a gun. A rabbit grazes nearby, and Sam is growing angry as Bobby repeatedly drops the gun before he can get off a single shot. Furious, Sam finally untangles his boy's hand and takes the gun away. Bobby is used to his father's anger, and he resumes pointing at the rabbit with his finger instead. In one smooth motion, his father stands tall with the pistol and fires. The rabbit explodes in a flash of blood, dust, and fur, and the Future Ranger blinks in shock at his father's lethal speed and casual cruelty.

***

Later that day, Sam and his son hover over a dozen weapons laid out on top of the display case in Sam's gun store. Sam is giving his son a fast history of each gun while moving him down the line to see if his small hands can wield just one pistol successfully.

"See these guns?" Sam asks. "These are my prize dozen. And they make my calendar, boy. I take one gun out each month and get to know it all over again. It helps me remember what month it is, too. Pay attention and one day you won't just be carrying no apple peeler."

He picks up what appears to Bobby to be the shell of an unfinished revolver.

"This is always my first gun of the year," he continues. "I take it out every January. It's called 'The Skeleton,' forged in 1880. All the springs and gears are visible, revealing that there ain't really much to guns after all. It was a prototype, created as an instructional tool to sell to the Mexican army. D.B. Wesson hisself made this creature so you could see all the organs working for the first time. Legend has it that this skeleton of a gun was fired into the skeleton of a dog, so that they could study the inside of the gun *and* the target simultaneously."

"They shoulda got a skeleton to shoot it, too!" Bobby laughs, reaching for the handle. But the Future Ranger's hand is too small for it, and Sam is snatching it away, more annoyed at his son's joke than the genetic failings of his grip.

"Pay attention to what I tell you about these weapons, boy. A lot of folks will tell you stories about how this gun did this and that bullet did that. All bullshit. I'm gonna give you the straight history right now..."

They move down. Sam holds up a long, strange pistol with a large row of teeth surrounding the cylinder in its center.

"February," he says. "This was the first .44. First made in 1870 and called the 'Model 3 American.' Has more kick than a Big Fifty Sharps, and almost as long. This weapon here was a prototype where the firing pin rotated instead of the cylinder. No more guessing what chamber had a bullet in it, if you were one of those boys that liked to spin it after loading. Or one of those fools who liked to guess. This particular gun killed 27 people the day it debuted... all during games of Russian Roulette."

Bobby smiles at his dad's attempt at humor, but Sam doesn't let him hold this particular gun either. They slide down the counter to pause in front of a large, silver revolver.

"March. This is the .45 Auto Loader, originally built for government testing. You can take it apart into pieces that can then be taken apart into smaller pieces and so on and so on and so forth. Do you like magic tricks, son? No? Good, because I hate them."

In a flurry of grunts and hand movements, he quickly dismantles and reassembles the weapon. Bobby starts to point out the several pieces remaining sprinkled across the counter after the reassemble, and Sam brushes them off onto the floor.

"When I was your age, I liked playing with this gun every March because that's when your grandpa would usually finish putting together the jigsaw puzzle he'd started during the winter. That always made sense to me. Especially because you don't have to put the pieces of a jigsaw puzzle back the way they want you. Your granddad taught me that."

"Daddy, did you say '1870'?" Bobby asks, glancing at the gun parts on the floor, then scratching at the wood on the corner of the gun case. There's a heart with a year carved inside it, a heart Bobby gouged into the counter a decade ago, but he suddenly realizes he got the year wrong back then. He's not sure, but he's now worried this may have screwed up his sense of time for good. He's not too worried though. He'd messed up the heart pretty bad, too. Although he'd heard once that a real heart *did* have three points on it, at least. And fingers. Kinda.

"Oh yeah, one more thing, boy. They say you can reduce this weapon down to small enough puzzle pieces that you could swallow it... if you had to. Of course, that particular feat don't mean too much. I saw a man eat a piano once. And I don't mean he 'bit the dirt,' I mean he really, truly devoured a baby grand from teeth to toes. Hell, a man could eat an entire gun factory if he just kept shittin'."

Bobby backs up a step.

"You hungry, boy?" he laughs.

"But it's not March, is it, Pa?" Bobby shivers, trying to change the subject. "It's too cold outside for March."

Sam squeezes his son's shoulder.

"Settle down now. What kind of father would force his son to eat a gun? Because a bastard like that should get some kinda reward!"

***

Dona Aña, New Mexico. 1895, present day.

Early morning, and the air's still cool. Tom kicks around the rusted remnants of an exploded weapon scattered in the dirt, as the Ranger sits on the ground nearby. The letter Tom delivered flaps with the wind, smacking the Ranger's knee for attention. The name on the envelope reads "Wendler" in large, child-like script.

"Ain't it a little early to be resting?" Tom asks. "On the road, no less?"

"Not really," the Ranger says. "March is the first official month for sitting your ass on the ground. 'Nobody marches in March,' my dad used to say. And last icicle shattered three weeks ago."

Tom circles him impatiently.

"Well, aren't you gonna read it?" Tom asks as he reaches down to pick up the rusted cylinder from a gun that exploded that morning, as well as decades before. "After I deliver mail to you on a *Sunday*?"

He flicks some dirt to reveal a piece of the revolver's hammer.

"You could probably salvage this thing," Tom says. "Not that anyone should want to. Hold on a second. What was this made out of?"

He picks up the shard and sniffs it.

"This ain't pig iron, is it?" he asks as he sniffs again. "The smelt went wrong when they made this, that's for sure."

The Ranger says nothing.

"You don't make guns outta this shit," Tom laughs, flicking it away like it's a dung shard and wiping his hands on his thighs. "So you gonna read the letter or what, boss?"

"Why don't you just tell me what it says," the Ranger says, still not looking up.

"I don't read your mail. I just bring it. On a *Sunday*. Of course, if it was open already..."

Now the Ranger raises his head.

"Well, it *was* open," Tom says, looking guilty. "It's from some sheriff's wife. She says that they won't have any more water in Agua Fría in about two weeks. Not one drop to drink."

"Well," the Ranger sighs. "That's two years longer than I thought that town would last."

"She says the wells are drying up," Tom says, talking fast now. "She says in two weeks anyone who ain't left town will be dead because she says it takes a week in every direction to get anywhere else. She says they have a bell tower in the town that's gonna chime when they're past the point of no return. She says when the bell tolls, it's too late to even try to leave. She says a lot of people are gone or going, but some people are staying, too. Including her."

"Whoa whoa. What? How long ago was the letter sent?"

"A week ago?" Tom shrugs. "That bell she's talking about probably started ringing today."

"Why the hell would anyone stay where there isn't any water?" the Ranger asks himself more than Tom, kicking a heel in anger.

"Oh, yeah, one more thing. She says there ain't any sheriff there anymore either. Ever hear of a man named 'Red'?"

Hearing this, the Ranger stands up, face furrowing into knuckles.

"But you ain't going there for him either. You're going for that sweet Angelica, am I right? Tell your sister I said hello."

The Ranger stares at Tom until Tom has to turn, then he starts collecting the pieces of his exploded revolver. Tom holds it in a while, but finally can't help but laugh, in spite of the beating he received last time he mocked the man.

"Yeah, don't forget your gun!"

***

Agua Fría.

A mob surrounds a burning church. A gaunt, frazzled preacher appears from the smoke to address a congregation standing dangerously close to the flames. The Preacher holds a large Bible high above his head as he launches into a sermon, eyes almost pinwheeling. Over his shoulder, the towering cross on the church's steeple shimmers, its own arms outstretched in the flames.

"Brothers and sisters, we are living in dangerous times. We are forced to gather here, outside the remnants of our doxology works, as it's getting to where everything in this town is dry enough to catch fire without warning. Including me. Including you. Now, there's going to be the urge to drink something, anything, with the water gone. I'm here to tell you that the water in your outhouse is better for you than any bottle. I know there's still plenty of whiskey around, and I know it seems like that's the answer. But it's not! Do not bend an elbow. Do not consume that fargin' coffin varnish. Drink the water from your outhouse instead is what I'm saying to you all. Amen."

The Preacher stops to hide his mouth behind his Bible. He's either laughing or sobbing, but he pulls it back together.

"I'll tell ya, if someone would have told me that I'd have said those words in a sermon when I was first getting sworn in..."

"They swear in lawmen, not preachers," a shriveled boy says to his mother, and she slaps him hard across the face. The rest of the crowd smiles at their leader, nervous but adoring. All of this angers the Preacher somehow.

"Let's get something straight. I know the Bible is full of them, but I think y'all are under the mistaken impression that I'm using metaphors or allusions here. I'm not saying that whiskey is bad by jokingly comparing it to drinking your own piss, like some fable, knowing that no one would ever really do that. That's not what

I'm saying. Listen close this time. Drinking the whiskey will kill you faster than drinking from the buckets we hang under our own asses."

Someone gasps. Someone else mutters, "He's right."

"Your body will die faster from whiskey than it would from ocean water," the Preacher says. "So I'm telling you, find the water that's left, no matter what the color, you shake the floaters out of it, and you drink deep!"

He studies the uncertainty on their dying faces.

"Okay, maybe start in the horse troughs, then move to the pigs, *then* check where it's dumped under your outhouse. Then check the buckets used to clean *those* buckets. Drink from these buckets and live!"

The crowd cheers.

"Also, I saw someone eating an apple today, my brothers and sisters. And even though this may seem like a good source of fluids, that just don't seem right. Do I have to even say it? Don't eat apples. Drink 'apple jack.' Amen."

An old woman in the back of the crowd raises her hand.

"Yes, sister."

"Didn't you say last Sunday that wasn't really an apple in the Garden of Eden? That it was our hearts? Or an artichoke heart? Something like that?"

"Sister, I've said a lot of things. But that was before the world ended. That was before every day was a Sunday. And I've had to rethink some things. So don't eat apples! Can I get an 'Amen'?"

The congregation mutters a half-ass "Amen" but looks more confused than ever. Satisfied with this result, the Preacher claps the Bible hard above his head and looks around.

"Now! Who knows any songs..." He cocks a thumb behind him to the burning church. "...because the goddamn hymnals were in there."

***

Dona Aña. Same day.

The Ranger stands in front of a line of young men, unrolling a stack of wanted posters. All of the men have one hand in the air and one hand over their heart. All except for one, that is. Tom McMaster, at the front of the line, is picking his ear with his raised hand. The Ranger glares at Tom a moment, decides he's not ready for the pledge, then slaps the roll of posters hard enough against Tom's chest to make him cough. The Ranger stretches one poster to read what he scribbled on the back years ago.

"'I will bear true allegiance to the State of New Mexico, and I will serve her honestly and faithfully against all her enemies, to observe and obey the orders of the Governor of our fine State, and the orders of the officers appointed over me, namely myself, according to a Congressional Act allowing the raising of a battalion for protection of the frontier, approved March 17th, sworn and subscribed before me this day of the 17th of March A.D. 1853, Robert Ford, New Mexico Mounted Patrol.'"

"Bob, it's not 1853," Tom whispers.

"Who gives a shit. Now say, 'I will,' you grubby bastards."

"I will!" most of them shout.

"Okay! You're all sworn in. We're out of badges, so go ahead make one if you want. Anything will do, really."

The men steal glances at each other, not sure if they believe him, and the Ranger impatiently waves them over.

"Well, don't just stand there. Come grab a poster. Plenty to go around. Then I'll need you to..."

He trails off, staring down at one filthy poster in the pile. The men shuffle anxiously, waiting for him to speak again, but he just motions them forward and flings the roll of posters to their feet. A pile of crude drawings of armed men scowling under various scrawled dollar amounts fans out wide across the dirt. The men quickly swarm and start grabbing, arguing over the highest rewards. The Ranger walks away from the mob stripping one poster from the top of the stack, like a shifty dealer skinning the best card for himself. Tom eyes him suspiciously and trots after him.

"Hey! What you got there? Keeping the buster money for yourself, huh?"

The Ranger catches Tom's grasping hand at the wrist, and with his other hand, he quickly folds the poster into a square to stuff away inside his coat.

"Don't ever grab for me like that, boy," the Ranger says, genuinely surprised.

"Relax, Bob. I just wanted to see how much that reward was. Is it more than five hundred? I haven't seen any posters more than five hundred. What's the big secret? How come you get to keep that one? Like I don't know already who that was."

The Ranger releases Tom and turns away. Tom stands rubbing his wrist, watching him walk off. Then he runs back to the men and the poster pile, the arguing now turning to shoving. The Ranger picks a jangling bag up off the ground and claps his dusty hands together to get everyone's attention again.

"Back in line, you fuckin' grangers! Grab your target and get the hell back in line!"

The men form their row again in the street, and the Ranger moves through the new rangers, handing out badges from his bag. The men eagerly pin them to their coats, eyes betraying minds already dropping bad guys and stacking money. Tom McMaster takes a badge from the Ranger, bends the corner with a tooth, then puts the tin star away in his pocket.

"I thought we weren't getting these yet. I thought we were supposed to make a better one out of a bird's nest or some shit? When did the real one's come in?"

"I still have the real ones. I figured you guys weren't ready. And you proved me right. But now I have to leave, so we're cuttin' lessons short. Good luck to ya."

"Where we goin'?" Tom shouts, and the line disperses again.

"Me? Agua Fría," the Ranger says, looking past him.

"Hmm, sounds familiar," Tom laughs. "Now, I heard that town's dry as bone. Hell, I hear even the mail don't run no more, not as good as it does here anyway. Must be a lot of money waiting for you out there, huh, boss?"

"There ain't nothing out there for you, Tom," the Ranger says slowly, and something in his eyes cuts Tom's laugh off at the knees. Then a loud voice comes from the back of the crowd.

"Bullshit!"

"Who said that?" someone wants to know.

"The man in back," Tom says.

"Did you say 'the man in *black*'?" someone wonders.

"No," Tom sighs. "The man in *back*."

Tom and the Ranger walk around the crowd until they come to a small man in the back of the crowd, actually wearing a little black band on his hat after all.

"You had something to say?" the Ranger asks.

"Well, I heard they found gold in Agua Fría after the first well ran dry," says the Man in Back. "In fact, I heard the gold's got something to do with those wells running dry, and that's why there's still people there." He points at the bulge in the Ranger's coat. "People worth a little money anyway."

"I heard that story, too," Tom smiles. "But I don't think it's gold our ol' Bob is looking for, is it, boss?"

The Ranger ignores both men and strides through the center of the crowd, then back through one more time. He searches their eyes with each step.

"I'm going to Agua Fría to swear in a new sheriff. And that's all you need to know."

"You're kinda big on this 'swearing' thing, ain't ya, boss?"

He angrily whirls around and reaches into Tom's pocket to pull out the badge he'd just given him. He opens the pin and jams the star into his coat over his heart. Then he pushes harder, and the men close enough to hear his skin pop trip over themselves to head somewhere else fast. Tom flinches in pain as the Ranger pulls his nose up toward his until they're both breathing the same dust.

"Yes. I am."

FOUR

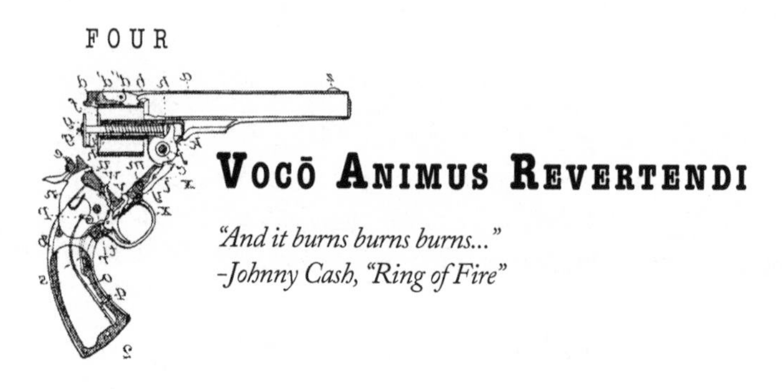

Vocō Animus Revertendi

"And it burns burns burns..."
-Johnny Cash, "Ring of Fire"

Agua Fría.

Twitchy and miserable, the gang watches as Red holds his branding iron over a blazing campfire. They wring their hats in their hands, faces pinched from the heat of the flames and their new inability to produce sweat. Red grabs one of them, Ned Parker, slandered throughout the town as variations of "Egg," by his shredded collar, and buries the glowing orange metal into his throat. Egg hisses in pain, but doesn't scream, as the iron peels away from his neck, taking bloody layers of sizzling chicken skin along with it. When the smoke clears from around Egg's head, the number "**13**," branded just below Egg's ear, is now visible flickering in the firelight. Red stands back to check out his handiwork, grinning and flipping the smoking iron around in his hand.

"And why did I just endure that again, Red?" Egg sighs, eyes still shut.

Red turns back to fire. He jams the iron in the flames again and studies his men to pick his next victim. He points to Al Mutters, the one they all call "Mud."

"Because you're a bad egg, Eggsucker, plain and simple!" Red says, playfully spinning the rod. "Mud, you're next. Wipe the dirt off your neck and the custard out of that Zapata. If you can. Got too many buckle bunnies to get through here."

Mud walks over, head down, leaning in to offer his neck like a submissive dog to its master. The scars of another brand line his collarbone, an especially painful "**G.T.T.**," left by his wife when he was dead drunk, to announce she'd gone to Texas with some other hard case.

"I think Egg raises a good question," he says, timid. "Why the hell do we need to... *Ah! Fuck!*"

Red sinks the brand into his neck, holding it at a different angle this time. When he pulls it back and waves away the smoke, only the number "**3**" is now readable.

"Next! You heard me, Jackass."

Jack Hicks steps forward and receives the branding iron at yet another angle. The number "**1**" is revealed burned into his throat. Because Egg, the scrawniest of the gang, didn't scream, none of the gang dares to call out.

"Next!"

Little Joe, the shortest member of the gang, a squat boy of about 15, is the last one to step forward. Red ruffles his hair affectionately before he pushes the red metal behind his ear, just under his hairline. The boy closes one eye but does not flinch, not even once. The men nod in respect, holding their aching heads. Red presses the brand the longest against the boy, and when the smoke clears, Little Joe's been branded with the number "**13**," just like Egg.

"You're more man than any of us, chickabiddy," Red tells him.

Egg angrily steps forward.

"Hey, hold on!" he says. "We're out of numbers. We got '**1**,' '**3**,' '**13**'... and '**13**.' How the hell's that gonna work?"

"Forget all that," Mud says through clenched teeth, gently tapping the angry burn on his neck with two fingers. "I know it's your birthday n' all, boss, but I think we deserve to know why we're letting you brand us like animals."

Red turns to look at Mud, glaring, jaw muscles fluttering. Then he relaxes and throws the smoking branding iron into the dirt and tries to sound convincing and leader-like.

"If you men are going to stay here in this dead-ass town and look for that gold with me, you're gonna start dyin'. That's just a fact, and there's no getting around that. This town has dried up, and from what they're sayin', once that bell rings, we're all gonna have about three days to live. Now, I'm gambling I can find that gold and ride out of here before I take the big jump. And you've all decided to take this gamble with me. Because you're stupid. But the problem is—and I realized this today after looking at all your fuckin' mugs too fuckin' long—is that after about two days, your faces are gonna be nothin' but skin stretched over skulls, a buncha dried apples on windowsills. And I ain't gonna be able to tell y'all apart! And it's goddamn hard enough as it is. Y'all look like identical walkin', squawkin' stacks of shit when you're healthy, let alone when yer dead. So, to make things easier, in case there's an emergency where I really need to know your fuckin' names, I thought I'd give you boys some numbers instead. Little *vocō*... *vocō* ... whatever-the-hell they call that shit. Get it?"

Red claps Egg hard on the back. The gang exchange glances.

"Good! And you of all people should be on board with this, Egg. Don't I see you putting your goddamn initials on every tree in this county? We're essentially talkin' about the same concept here."

Egg's eyes flash in anger, but he drags them reluctantly toward the ground.

"Don't you ever look at me like that, Egg. You should have hearn my first three ideas about how to keep track of all of you fuckers. Ever see a dog with its ears bobbed?"

Red pulls a knife from his belt and reaches over to flick Egg in the ear. Egg jumps back rubbing his neck and tugging his earlobe to make sure it's still there.

"Or a 'Bob' with his ears 'dogged'?" Red laughs at his own joke. "And think of it this way. Any of you get lost and forget where you are, someone will return you to me. I think it's a law. In fact, I know it's a law. It's all Latin and shit, but I can't invoke it when I've been drinking. But it means, 'With intention to eat!' Or 'return,' one of the two. We're together to the end, boys."

"Mm-hmm. I get all that," Egg says. "But you still got two

number '**13**s.' This just don't make no sense, but I guess you're the big mugwump 'round here."

Red loses some patience.

"And how long do you think I'll have two number '**13**s.'?" he shouts.

"As long as that little high binder lasts," Egg says, nodding nervously at Little Joe. "*I* ain't goin' nowhere." Little Joe crosses his arms, defiant, and Egg nods again. "And how can his name be 'Little Joe' when there ain't no fuckin' 'Big Joe' anywhere?"

Red studies him a moment, then walks slowly towards Egg, and, in a quick burst of motion, tackles him and screws his face painfully into the dirt.

"Egg, you've convinced me. Now, lest you want me to declare you *ferae naturae* instead, hold the fuck still."

After a few seconds of Egg puffing dust, Red twists his head sideways to expose the raw, angry brand on his neck. Then he waves the kid over.

"Little Joe! Come here."

The kid runs to him, and Red hands him the knife, still crouching on a terrified Egg's chest. Red squints and studies the number on his neck, cocking his head a bit, deep in thought.

"Now, I'm thinking... if you take the '**3**'... cut another '**3**' backward over top of it... you should get something like an '**8**.' See how deep you can cut without killing... oh, shit. Sorry 'bout that."

Egg screams as the tip of the blade sinks into his throat.

***

A mile away and an hour later, a line of people walk their foaming horses and filthy belongings past the remains of a courthouse as they head out of town. The sluggish, emaciated animals are overloaded with bags, clothes, and equipment, while weary families scrape alongside looking lost, hopeless. A skinny, black dog slinks behind everyone, circling heels, sniffing for food. Someone kicks at the dog in anger, and it backs off for a moment, then creeps back to their shuffling feet. It begins snorting around the dust kicked up by a short, toothless man as Little Joe comes around a storefront corner and yells at the long line of marching townspeople. Red's Mexican woman is skittering behind the dog, carrying a dead, gray baby. Mercifully, it's upside down so no one can get lost in its sunken eyes.

"Why bother leaving now? The bell ain't rung yet!" Little Joe yells at the crowd. "Horses already baked, and I don't see no Adam's Ale where you're headed! Hey, did you see that kid's marbles?"

"My water's walking right alongside me, boy," Toothless says, patting the nearest dying horse. "If this beast makes it halfway, then I can sure as hell make it the other half."

"Hold on," Little Joe says, tilting his hat and scratching his sun-baked scalp. "You talking about drinking a horse?"

"Times like these, we have to start using words a little different," Toothless says, walking on. "Expanding their meaning, you might say. Think of it that way, and you can drink whatever you want."

A wicked understanding seems to dawn on Little Joe, and he sprints up to the man's horse, draws his gun and fires. The horse staggers, then falls over. Toothless jumps back in terror, almost like he expects it to burst into kindling when it hits the ground.

"You can't drink a horse, you crazy bastard!" Little Joe yells. "That's cruel!"

The toothless man blinks in shock at his dead animal, then notices the dog slinking around in his peripherals. He clicks his tongue to get it to come over, then pets it a bit to slow his heart back down. When he starts walking again, the dog starts walking next to him, and together they avoid Little Joe's eyeballs until the kid safely puts away his iron. But when they get close, Little Joe sighs and grabs the scruff of the dog's neck to stop it in its tracks.

"Naw, you're staying here, boy," he says. "Crazy bastards will try to drink you, too. Never trust a man that thirsty."

FIVE

Cocking Fingers

"He points to the sky and says, 'The sun's not yellow, it's chicken.'"
-Bob Dylan, "Tombstone Blues"

Dona Aña. "Mourning."

The Ranger is hunched forward on a stool with a doctor crouched in front of him and leaning in close. The doctor backs up to stare with his arms crossed, leans in close again, then backs up to stare at him with his arms locked back up, fingers drumming on his forearm.

"I'm sorry, Bob, you're in a bad box," the doctor says. "I give you about three weeks."

At this, the Ranger stands and walks to the nearest window. He stares at a featureless skyline for three full minutes, then abruptly slaps his hat on his knee and heads for the door through the swirl of dust he created. Those three minutes are the longest he's ever felt sorry for himself in his life, and this disgusts him. So he's talking about a couple things when he responds.

"It's more time than I need."

***

The Ranger drags his heavy barn doors open one at a time. The doors are rotten and sagging, and they dig long trenches in the dirt as he struggles. Finally, he's spread them wide enough to step inside. He looks his horse up and down, blinking slow as his eyes adjust. It's a young, black Mustang, neighing and pacing restlessly, anxious to be loosed. Seeing him, it stops, snorts and sprays him with mucus, then lets loose a long stream of urine in the Ranger's direction. The Ranger sighs and waits for it to finish, then he grabs a saddle and starts heading towards the beast. The horse's eyes roll around like pool balls on the break, and when the Ranger is behind it, its tail lifts, serving up a long log of feces that swirls and wraps around the horse's back leg like a huge cake decoration. The Ranger drops the saddle in disgust and defeat.

"Explain to me again why there's so many songs about you goddamn crowbaits," he mutters.

He taps his pocket watch and notes the time, then picks the saddle back up and throws it over the Mustang's back. After a couple slips and muttered curses, he's saddled it and mounted. He spits at a spot of dirt on its neck and roughly rubs a burr from its tangled mane as he leads it outside. They squint up at the sun together and recoil. It's the last time they'll agree on anything.

***

Agua Fría. Same day.

The distant, ominous sound of a church bell echoes through the farmhouse. McKenna Wendler, a weary, middle-aged but attractive woman, is standing in front of a large, open chest at the foot of her bed. It's empty, except for a framed picture turned upside down. She rights it and stares thoughtfully. Her nine-year-old boy, Robby, runs in right then with a handful of wooden toys and hops around next to her, full of energy. He's a small, healthy, reddish-brown-haired child in an oversized shirt, a little hyper but smiling, respectful. For the moment. After shuffling his feet impatiently, he nudges his mother with a shoulder.

"Ain't we packin', Ma? This is all my things. Where's your things?"

McKenna doesn't speak, then turns from the photograph to look at her boy.

"Go ahead and keep playing with those toys, son. We're not leaving."

She closes the now-empty chest, and Robby drops everything except for a splintering, wooden toy gun. He sees the picture she's holding and reaches for it, and half a black, dead rose that was hanging from where it curled around the corner of the frame falls to the floor between them.

"That Pa?" Robby asks.

"Yes," she says, hesitating. "That's your father."

"He'd have made us leave quick," Robby says. "We'd have gone yesterday."

"Yeah, you're probably right."

The boy pulls the picture in her hand closer so he can study it. It's a blurry, sepia tone photo of a stern-looking man wearing a two-gun rig and a gleaming sheriff's badge. Scrawled on the photo is the word "Gray" in childlike script.

"How come daddy was named after a color?"

"Don't you remember? You named him."

"Huh?"

"You wrote 'Gray' instead of 'Gary' on this picture when you were five years old. And he liked it so much, the name stuck. He said it made more sense than we knew. You know that story, now don't act like you don't just so I'll tell it again!" she smiles.

"How'd he die?"

"What did I just say about pretending you don't know things?" McKenna says, suddenly angry. "You know that answer. You were there. Why do you want to keep hearing about such things? Why do you keep acting like it didn't—"

She calms herself and sets the picture down on a table. There's a loud knock on their door, and she waits to answer it since her face is flushed. But before she or Robby can respond, Red slams the door open against the wall, and strides into their house like he owns it.

"Why the hell haven't you left?" Red asks her, shaking his head. "Can't you hear the goddamn bell?"

"Get out," McKenna says, clocking all other exits.

"Why don't we go see the elephant, friends!" he says. "Hit the groggery for one last drink."

Robby points his toy gun at Red's face, glaring through one eye as he aims it, and Red smiles.

"Holy hell! Your boy's the first creature I've seen in this town in weeks that's healthy enough to look so furious!" He looks around the room, then adds. "Why is that, I wonder?"

McKenna slaps the door with her hand, sending it swinging back.

"I said to get out."

Red doesn't move.

"No, *I* said to get out, remember?" He notices the chest nearby and scowls, suspicious. He quickly kicks it open and sees that it's empty, frowning in disbelief, convinced he's missing something. Always missing something.

"Out," she says, firm.

"Well, goddamn," Red says, smiling wider. "I take it back. *Two* healthy creatures."

He turns to leave, but stops at the door as he notices Gray's picture on a table. He picks it up, and his features narrow in hate. He side-arms the picture against the wall, shattering the image in an explosion of glass.

"You still don't know what the fuck he was up to, do ya?" he says. "Nobody knows the truth about that man. 'Cept me. And nobody asks me shit."

Robby moves to slide the photograph from under the broken shards, keeping his toy gun carefully aimed at Red all the while. Robby slowly moves a thumb like he's cocking the toy, and they stare each other down. The church bell rings in the distance five more times, then stops. Red turns to McKenna.

"You hear that? Me neither!" He wags a finger at them. "Listen to me now. Time's up. Pack your shit and leave, or you'll be dead in three days. Or maybe you're the first person in history that don't need water?"

He nods at the picture in the boy's hand.

"I know you don't need anything else, huh, kid?"

Something outside draws his attention, and he cranes his head toward their back door.

"Or maybe it's those horses out there in your barn? I know you're hiding horses. You afraid to leave them show ponies to dry up? Is that all this is?"

He turns back to Robby, who still has Red in his sights. Smiling big at the boy, Red slowly reaches towards McKenna to flick a droplet of water off the end of her nose.

"Boy, did you know your mama here is the only person around town healthy enough to bleed water? Everyone else is sweating sand and smoke out there, right now as we speak. But not you two. No, you're all healthy and mad... and she's sweating! It's just like any other day around this house, ain't it?"

Big, big smile. Robby's toy gun wavers a second, then lowers slightly.

"Why are you named after a color?" Robby asks him.

"Ask your Ma," Red says, nodding at her, then back at Robby. "Son, you got to be careful with that thing. Don't you know a toy gun can kill?"

In a flash, Red is suddenly pointing his finger at the boy. Then he cocks his thumb like a hammer. Robby and McKenna flinch, thinking for a moment that he actually drew a weapon. McKenna isn't sure of the difference between the two in a situation like this.

"Fingers can be just as dangerous!" Red says. "Don't need no barking irons at all. Remember, it's our hands that do the killing, not the toys."

His smile stretches even wider as he swipes the wooden gun from out of Robby's hands and turns to walk out, tucking the toy gun into his belt. Robby reaches down and picks up the dead rose from off the picture. Nostrils flaring in hate, he begins to pluck the biggest thorns from its stem and stuff them into the deep pockets of his oversized shirt.

***

Edge of town. Hours later.

Jackass and Mud watch townsfolk ride past them, fascinated that families of blacks, Indians, and Mexicans make up most of the caravan.

"Check out them exodusters," Mud says.

"You know why they're leaving and we're staying?" Jackass asks.

"Why?"

"I'll tell ya. Because the only documented cases of suicide in the history of the world are by white people."

Mud looks skeptical, even more skeptical when he spots Red approaching from the distance, weaving his horse towards them like he doesn't have a care in the world.

"That ain't true," Mud says. "Is that true?"

"Is what true?" Red asks.

"Only whites kill theyselves."

"Hell, yeah, that's true!" Red laughs. "Check any newspaper or gospel mill. Or even the Bible for that matter."

Red starts to smile, and quickly draws and points a weapon at Mud's eye. Mud's eye twitches and flinches, then opens back when he sees Red holding a wooden toy gun instead of his Colt Peacemaker, a.k.a. his "Piece Taker." Red tosses the toy to Mud, then aims his finger at Mud's other eye, which now twitches and flinches even more severely.

"What did you think was gonna come out of my finger? Close your mouth, tongue-foot."

"Can't help it."

"Well, me neither," Red says, laughing even harder.

***

A couple miles away, Robby kicks his way through a dead cornfield, looking for something he lost long ago. He kicks at half-buried rocks and stumbles when one doesn't move aside like the rest. Crouching down, he wrestles loose a large stone and rolls it away, then he pulls a smaller stone out of the hard dirt underneath it. This second stone is oddly pointed and shaped remarkably like a small revolver. He picks it up, squeezes the mud around its handle, holding it in his tiny hand at arm's length, pointing his rock at the sun, wondering why men always closed one eye to aim.

SIX

The Man Who Hated Horses

"You know the shit that used to work? Well, it won't work now."
-Warren Zevon, "My Shit's Fucked Up"

Bisbée, New Mexico. 12:03 p.m.

The Ranger is riding past the long-shuttered storefronts of a small, dead town. It's dark and overcast, rain regularly threatening but never falling. He passes a rundown gun store, the dirt on its windows revealing it as decades out of business. The Ranger dismounts in front of the front door, trying to keep his nervous horse from agitation. They struggle a while anyway, and eventually the Ranger gives up and watches the horse trot away, shaking its head and snorting. He walks around the gun store and comes to a small shack attached to the back wall, a light flickering in the one window that's been wiped clear. He looks inside, sees no one, then opens the door. The Ranger's father, Sam Ford, a grizzled old man looking every minute of 180 years, sits on a bucket, cleaning the cylinder of a pistol with a pipe cleaner. Sam sighs "Bob," almost under his breath, but doesn't look up to greet his son.

"Hey, dad," the Ranger says, feeling more like "Bob" again and less like a ranger every new second. "How's business?"

"Smartass."

"Sorry, couldn't help it." Bob looks around the shack. "Can't imagine why you're closed though. The guns you gave me always shot straight as rain."

Sam does look up at this comment, a smile cracking the crags of his face.

"I didn't hear you come up," he says. "You walk across the desert barefoot?

Bob laughs and moves some crates and bags of beans to sit down.

"Yeah, you heard us out there fighting, huh? Still riding that goddamn horse. You're lucky I can't blame you for that relationship, too."

"Go ahead if you want," his father says. Then, "You know, boy, you've never had any respect for horses. All your life. Yet all around you, everyone else learns to work with those creatures. Ride 'em, feed 'em, depend on 'em. Not you. I shoulda got you some oxbows and pancakes when you were little, train you to appreciate how riding is so much easier now."

Bob traces a couple lines in the dust with his toe, then crosses his arms.

"Listen, I've only had two or three of them things, each one worse than the last. Maybe I'd care more if I traveled more, if I had anywhere I wanted to go. But as it stands, this hoss is the worst I've ever rode. I didn't even name it because I was afraid if it had a name, then I'd think about it even more. And then I'd have to kill it."

"You'll never understand the problem, boy. A man needs a horse that's more like him. Once you do that, you'll change your tune and not have such a fit sitting up in the hurricane deck."

"Not likely."

Sam looks his son up and down, nodding at his bandaged hand and laughing.

"Which, in your case, means you need a horse with three legs, no balls, and one eye."

The Ranger claps an affectionate hand on his father's shoulder, and some tension is broken.

"Why are you here? You ain't headed for Agua Fría are ya?"

Bob turns away from the question, heading for a window like he's apt to do.

"'Cause if you are, she ain't there no more. Nobody's there no more. That town dried up last year."

"I hear there's some people still there with the guttersnipes."

"I doubt that. Unless they're the kind of people that don't need water."

Bob turns back towards him, and his dad laughs.

"That what you're looking for? Some half-lizard or some other fabrication! I'm right, ain't I? You looking to serve justice on some lizards."

Sam trails off as something seems to dawn on him. He snaps the cylinder shut and squints up at his son, suddenly understanding what brought him to town.

"Red's still there, ain't he? Is that what this is all about? He finally gave you a good enough reason."

"He's a wanted man."

"Uh huh. Yeah, well, that was always going to happen eventually. He just had to be put in the right set of circumstances for his true colors to shine. He finally killed someone?"

"More than someone." Bob's back to the window looking at dark thunderclouds that only tease the dying crops.

"That ain't rain. I know, it sure looks like rain. But clouds are stained black these days is all. Too much smoke in the world and too little water. It'll always look like rain, even when you're on fire."

"He killed Gray," Bob says, turning back. Sam considers this a moment.

"I guess he figured he'd stay and be king in a kingdom of lizards?"

"You know what they say. In the land of the blind, the one-eyed lizard is king."

"Well, what about her?"

"She's still there, too. And the boy. And more people than we know, I'm guessing."

"But what can you do, Bobby?"

"They need a new sheriff."

"What? They need a new sheriff? Is that supposed to be some kinda joke? For how long? A day? Even if there's anyone left out there right now, there won't be by the time you ride in."

"Yeah, well, Red might have been waiting for a chance to run things at the end of the world, but I've also been waiting for him to do that very thing."

The Ranger turns to leave, but Sam gets in front of the door to block his way.

"Boy..." he starts.

"Daddy, you can't still call me 'boy' just 'cause you're the only person on Earth older than me."

"Soon to be the only person on Earth at all. That's exactly why I still call you 'boy,'" Sam says, then he grabs Bob's arm. "Listen to me, boy, you can't beat him. He's the fastest I ever saw. Fastest *you* ever saw. The only reason the world didn't notice it is because he wasn't a killer before. But it sounds like that's all changed now."

Bob tries to shove past.

"He ain't that fast," he says.

"You know he is."

Bob shoulders his father up against the door frame and walks out.

"Hey! You gonna see your Uncle Ron while you're here?" Sam calls after him. "He ain't got much time left, you know?"

"I don't know. Maybe," Bob says, looking up and down the road for his horse. "I just keep thinking, if I was dying, would I want anyone to come see me?"

"You're dying," his dad laughs. "And you came to see me! You always did shit backwards."

Bob ignores this, walking around the shack now.

"You seen that goddamn horse?"

"You don't even remember where your Uncle Ron lives, do you?"

"Of course I do!" Bob shouts. "He had the only tornado shelter in town. I still remember everyone down there underground. The adults playing cards under a lamp. Me and the kids shivering in the corner, listening to the wind outside. You guys never were afraid."

"Yeah, we were. We just never showed it."

Bob walks around the corner, yelling back over his shoulder.

"Hey, Pa! Find me a gun by tomorrow when I ride out. One that works this time!"

Sam laughs and turns around, muttering to himself again.

"Agua Fría, huh, Bob? You're really going back. Same as walking into the desert barefoot."

Bob is out of sight now, whistling for the horse, while Sam keeps the conversation going alone.

"You know what the name of that town means, boy? 'Cold Water.' And that's fuckin' funny since it's never had neither. Kind of like a Celestial holy man calling himself 'Johnny No God.' You hear me?"

He closes the door and sits back down in the dark, listens to the rumble of thunder that promised no relief.

"Son, you're gonna find things aren't the way you left them."

SEVEN

Hi, Johnny No God

"Born 200 years too late or 200 years too soon…
Will they marvel at the miracles I did perform and the heights I did aspire? Or will they tear out the pages of my book to light a fire?"
-Johnny Cash, "The Folk Singer"

Agua Fría.

The Preacher is sharing a tent with a half dozen members of his congregation, in the middle of another feverish, frantic sermon. He's up to three a day. His followers perch hangdog on a line of wooden crates, heads down and shoulders slumped like the living dead. The Preacher holds his Bible up high.

"I was reading a certain book the other day, and I noticed its spine was getting weaker."

He bends and twists the cover of his Bible back and forth, open then closed. The book cracks and pops, slivers of the leather binding fluttering down around his feet like ash.

"I never thought I'd be able to do this with such a big book, but with no moisture in the air, and everything else turning to dust, brothers and sisters, it seems I'm stronger than I've ever been."

In a grunt of effort, the Preacher tears the Bible completely in half. The zombies on the crates blink in shock, while the Preacher looks at the half of the book in his right hand, then throws it over his shoulder. With both hands, he holds the remaining half up over his head.

"This. This is all we need."

He opens the remaining pieces of his Bible and begins to read aloud from the Old Testament.

"'*You will plant vineyards and cultivate them but you will not drink the wine or gather the grapes because the worms will eat them...'"*

He stops, pulling a bottle of whiskey from his back pocket and taking a long swig.

"Do you know what this is? This is the Curse of Disobedience! But I'm here to say, I'm drinking the wine because it's the only thing left to drink! And I sure don't see any God stopping me."

He takes another long drink.

"All of you now, look down under your seats and you'll see a bottle where the hymnals used to be, well, I mean, down where the pews used to be... where a church used to be. Grip tight what you find. Come on! Take a drink. Drink and disobey Him, but do not disappoint."

The congregation looks around at each other, then reaches between their knees to find a bottle for each of them, just as he promised. They drink in silence, tiny beads of sweat rolling down the stubble and cracks in their faces like piss through sandpaper, warm whiskey dribbling down dusty chins to chase it.

"Good. Drink deep, children," he says, opening the half Bible again. "Now where were we... oh, yes. The Curse..."

The Preacher is consumed with coughs, and he tries in vain to clear his throat, hacking up a brown ball of mud and mucus instead.

"Swarms of locusts will take over all your trees and the crops of your land!" he continues, pointing at the blob, gravel-voiced.

At that moment, Red and Little Joe pull up the end of the tent and step inside. They look around at the gathering, fascinated.

"I told ya there were some dumb fucks still here!" Little Joe shouts. "They'd follow this converter anywhere."

"I hope not!" the Preacher laughs, waving them in, Bible flapping and dropping verses all over his scrawny arms.

Little Joe takes off his hat out of respect, and Red cuffs him for it.

"You boys lost?" the Preacher asks them.

They look at each other, then at him. Little Joe shrugs.

"Well, then you came to the right place!"

***

Bisbée. Same day. Same hour.

The Ranger stands in front of a two-story farm house, leaning on the last loose post from a fence long gone. His horse wanders off behind him, the strap from its halter dragging through the brittle grass. He sees a shadow in one of the windows and starts to walk to the porch, but stops, then walks, hat and head down, past the house instead and into the backyard. He searches the field until he finds a trap door grown over with weeds. He crouches and takes his hat off, seemingly paying his respects to this hole in the ground. Then he pulls a horseshoe handle with a grunt to open the hatch with a suck of dust swapping the outside air, and he looks down into the dark. Wind whistles up from the depths of his uncle Ron's tornado shelter, and he breathes the cold wind and damp earth of the tunnel for a few minutes. Then the Ranger puts his hat back on and stands, suddenly unsure of himself. He looks off in the distance and sees his horse, then looks the other way and sees another horse, this one with the shadow of a man on it, holding his own horse still as he watches to see what the Ranger does next. He stares a moment, sees the shadow tip a stovepipe hat, then looks back down into the dark, wrinkling his nose at a stench rising from the hole. Then, fast as a slap, a smooth green grass snake slips out of the hole and traces the seams in the trapdoor's hinges like a signature. The Ranger shudders. But only when the snake finds the Ranger's boot and starts working its head into the cracks above the heel does he jump back to let the door slam shut.

***

Agua Fría.

The latest dark sermon has ended, and outside of the church tent a smiling man does magic tricks for the dying crowd. The posts of the tent have collapsed to one side, and a scrurvy, tired-eyed boy watches the performance of exaggerated high steps and faked surprise as boots slide off his skeletal ankles.

"Whoa! How'd that happen?" asks Smiling Man, holding one boot up for the boy to see. He turns it upside down and shakes out some dirt.

"As y'all can see... nothing in my belly or my boot!"

The boy blinks, bored as Red and Little Joe walk up unnoticed behind Smiling Man. They watch him, amused as he does some more dramatic motions with his hands over the shoe and then pulls a twitching Leopard Gecko from inside the boot. The boy finally raises his hand.

"So, how'd you do that trick, mister?"

"It ain't no trick. Pay attention, you merry bucha b'hoys and g'hals. Miracles *can* happen."

When Red hears the word "miracle," his eyes narrow, and in a flash he pulls his revolver and a gaping bullet hole explodes between the man's eyes before he can finish his inspirational thought. He collapses forward, head leaking into the corners of his still smiling lips. The boy's eyes are wide, pupils black. Then he starts clapping.

"Now *there's* a magic trick for ya!" Red says, genuinely thankful for the applause.

A flap of ragged tent rises, and the Preacher steps out to survey the scene. He stares down at Smiling Man, only half smiling now as the synapses in his brain start misfiring.

"Why'd you do that, son?" he asks Red, hand over his heart.

"'Cause he wouldn't admit it was a trick. He was trying to say it was a miracle. That silly shit scares the children."

"What children?" the Preacher asks, frowning, palms out.

"That children," Red says, turning. "Why don't you ask him where his mother is?" Red looks around for the boy who was clapping and discovers him gone, no evidence of his visit. The Preacher turns to walk away, but Red grabs his arm.

"Hold it, jackeroo. Ain't you gonna at least say something?"

"Say something? Like what?" He stares back at the body. It's not even half-smiling anymore. "No, you were absolutely right. There are no miracles here."

Red lets his arm go, and the Preacher ducks back under the tent, dropping something in the process. Before Red can move to check it out, Robby Wendler pops back up from around a busted crate and runs to see what the Preacher left behind. Excited, he shakes the dirt out of a substantial piece of the New Testament and stuffs it in his front shirt pocket, then tears ass for home. Little Joe watches him go, then takes a step forward to pick up something, too. It's the black-and-yellow spotted gecko from the magic trick. He holds it up to the sun and squints at the lizard, finding its imitation of a smile infectious.

"Look at that! You can see right through its head!"

Red misunderstands and thoughtfully kicks some dirt onto the dead man's face to fill the bloody tunnel through his skull.

"Must be going around."

***

Bisbée. Dusk.

Tom McMaster stands next to his horse, a brown Appaloosa, as he stares down at the tornado door in an overgrown field. He looks one way, then the other, then, heart thrumming, he kicks at the horseshoe handle on the hatch leading into the ground. Then he looks up and down the horizon, scratching his neck. Too nervous to pull open the door, he walks back to his horse, climbs up, and rides away.

***

Hours later.

Tom walks into a bar and slaps a coin down on the counter in front of him. Without a word or a sideways glance, the bartender brings him a bottle of whiskey and scoops up the money.

"Whoa,"Tom says."A whole bottle? Joy juice is sure cheap around here."

"Gets even cheaper the further west you go," the bartender says without turning. "Go far enough, they might even start paying you to drink it."

"No shit."

Tom laughs and takes a swig as the bartender works on a brown blood stain on one end of the bar. After a moment, Tom knocks his knuckles on the counter for the bartender's attention.

"Hey, hello. You seen an Arizona Ranger come through here? Big, self-righteous-looking ape?"

"Nope."

Tom takes another drink, lets it sit a second.

"Okay, maybe you know anyone name of 'Red' 'round here instead."

"Which way you from again?" the bartender asks, standing up straight to work a cramp out of his elbow from the scrubbing.

Tom points to the left.

"Which way you going?"

Tom points to the right.

"He's two weeks that way."

Tom smacks two more coins on the bar, but the bartender turns back to his bloodstain, continuing to talk at him out the side of his neck.

"Keep 'em. If you're lookin' for Red, you'll need those for your eyes."

EIGHT

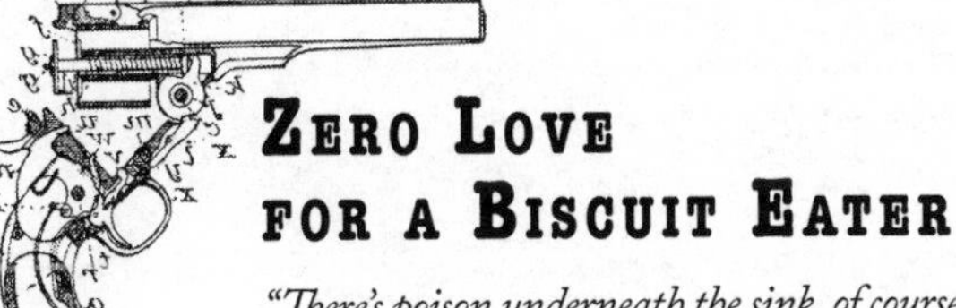

Zero Love for a Biscuit Eater

"There's poison underneath the sink, of course.
There's also enough formaldehyde to choke a horse."
-Tom Waits, "What's He Building In There?"

Agua Fría. Still now.

Red's gang are milling around in the dark, impatient for action. Egg walks up out of the shadows, rubbing the deep slashes around his neck.

"Holy shit! It's alive!" Mud shouts.

"Fuck off," Egg mumbles.

"Come here, Egg," Red says, waving him over. "Let me see what you got there."

Angry red gashes around his throat reveal the new number that Red has scarred him with, "**8888888888888**" in decreasingly deep burns as the brand cooled off on his skin.

"Hmmm. Yeah. Looks like Little Joe got a little carried away. But, hey, you wanted to be different! The number '**13**' wasn't good enough, remember?"

"Why do they call you 'Egg'?" Little Joe wants to know.

"Because that's my name."

"No," Red corrects him. "That wasn't your name until you got caught sucking eggs." He turns to Little Joe. "You know how 'Joe' is short for 'Joseph'? Well, 'Egg' is for 'Eggsucker'!"

Red finds this especially funny, so Mud finishes the story.

"People in this town killed three dogs for stealing eggs. Until they found out it was him."

"How'd he get caught?"

"Someone saw him take a dump with so many eggshells in it, they thought he was crapping out a deck of cards!" Red cackles.

"None of this is true," Egg says.

"The hell it ain't," Jackass shouts. "Naw, that boy is a biscuit eater. Don't let him lie about that. He can lie about everything else, but not that. They get zero love in this world."

"In spite of it all, we like to keep him around," Red says, still laughing. "Even though he's skinny and weak, he is dangerous. You know why? It's all them egg shells. You ever come across a dog straining to shit out some chicken bones? You ever try to pet that dog in the middle of it? Yeah, our Egg, he's hurting, but he'll still bite ya. He's a gooooood boy!"

"Hold on, when did who eat a deck of cards?" Mud asks.

"Hey, Egg, don't worry about your neck," Red says, slapping it hard. "It looks tough, like an old rope burn. Like someone tried to lynch your ass." He claps Egg on the back, softer. "Now come on before I give you a lacing. Let's go steal some shit."

A half hour later, Red and his gang are creeping around a dark farmhouse. A dead horse lies in the doorway of the nearby barn, a buzzard neck deep working a hole in its groin. The men sneak up to the porch, and Red slowly slides open a window and climbs inside. The gang peers in to watch Red walk around and scratch up under his hat awhile. Then he stomps back and climbs on out. He shoulders past the gang to the porch and savagely kicks down the front door. Clomping inside, Red lights a lamp, sits down in a rocking chair, and sighs loudly. The men cautiously file inside the splintered doorway.

"What's wrong, boss?" Mud asks, hat in hand. "Nothing to steal?"

"No, there's plenty to steal," Red sputters around his first existential dilemma. "Just no one to steal it from, so what's the point?"

***

Bisbée. Dusk.

Sam Ford veers uneasily down a dirt road, stopping every few feet to kick around the wagon tracks as if he's looking for something. Behind him, a man on a horse hides in the sun's glare, dismounting and trotting up before Sam can shield his eyes and assess the situation. When the man is close enough to recognize Sam, he flicks his hat up with a thumb so that the sun lights up his face. It's Tom McMaster, smiling with his mouth open from being out of wind. Sam notices the look of desperation on him, and turns to keep walking.

"Mr. Ford? Hello, sir, I'm one of your son's men, and we are supposed to rendezvous."

"Why'd you jump off your horse?"

"I guess I didn't want to startle you."

"The only way you could startle me, boy, is if you walked up here on your hands juggling skulls with your feet. Then maybe. I heard you coming three miles back."

"I see. Anyhow, I was looking for your son, Bob. See, we're supposed to be heading to..."

"Already come and gone."

Tom looks down and kicks some stones with the old man, trying to figure out what he lost.

"Did Bob grow up around here, sir?"

"Why?" Sam asks, finally looking long at Tom.

"Then you must know Red, too."

Sam picks up his pace.

"If you're looking for Red, you're lost, maybe you just oughta gig that horse and head home. You're 250 miles from Agua Fría. That's where Red is. Red's mother still lives here though. Used to anyway. Red and his ma came from Texas, actually. Anyone with red hair, they got it in Texas where you can still fuck an orangutan without a marriage license. They shoulda went back."

"I hear you got kin there, sir."

Sam looks at him harder, and Tom is suddenly sure he's about five seconds from being in real danger. He changes he subject.

"How about Gary Wendler?" Sam stops when he hears the name.

"You must know what happened to the sheriff, right?"

"Listen to me closely. I don't know what happened to Gray. I don't know what happened between him and her and all that. All I know is what happened between Red and my son."

Sam points to a tree nearby where one huge limb is cracked and hanging dead. A long, thin strip of bark is the only thing still connecting it to the tree. Tom walks up to it.

"Okay, you want the tour? We're in the perfect spot! You see that old, broken branch? That's where the fight started. But before it got to this tree, my boy knew Red was coming and he went out to ambush him. I let him pick out any gun he wanted from my store. Any gun! Do you know how much some of my guns are worth? Bobby didn't know it then, but it really didn't matter which gun he chose." He starts to reach down for something, but changes his mind. "Anyhow, apparently something went wrong with someone's gun, and it turned into a fist fight. The longest, ugliest lambasting this town never saw. That busted branch there? This one right here? That's where Red threw a punch and missed."

Tom kicks at the dead branch until it breaks loose, then turns it over with his boot to reveal the letters "**E.G.G.**" carved deep into the wood. Below that, another half-ass carving of "**G.T.T.**" Sam glares at him for casually destroying this landmark, but Tom's confusion makes him oblivious to his anger.

"So, hold on. Tell me, why did—"

"Both boys rode in at either end of town, and they met right here," Sam says impatiently, stamping a foot. "At this moment, you are standing on the exact geographical center of this town."

"Damn. So there never was any gun fight?"

"What the hell did I just say? Yes, that is right. There was a fist fight. There was a gun fight. Might have been a knife fight. Just because there's a gun fight, doesn't mean anybody gets shot. And, even though the outcome was violent, I must admit some relief that no one fired a shot into this particular leafless tree. See, my son was set to bushwhack him. And that would have made him a murderer. And even back then, and even though they got knocked galley west, and even though this isn't some rank shithole like Texas, he would have hanged for that."

The two men keep walking awhile. Sam keeps kicking around stones and dust, and Tom keeps watching him do it. The sun is long gone past the horizon, and Tom turns to look for his horse but can't see it in the dark. He slaps a fly away, frustrated.

"Where are you going anyway?" Tom asks. "You lose something?"

"Yes. I lost my brother."

Sam picks up his pace, no longer kicking around the stones. He points to a cracked orange boulder near the road.

"See the blood on that rock?"

"Yeah."

"The fight ended right there."

Startled, Tom looks around until he can estimate how long they walked past the tree with the broken branch. Almost a mile back down the road, he sees his horse sniffing the ground after them. The tree is somewhere past that.

***

Agua Fría. Same night.

Egg sits in a railroad shack, hunched over a crate with a carefully arranged spiral of split eggshells. Chicken eggs, vultures' eggs, crows' eggs, even some lizard eggs, all arranged by size and color along two of the three windowsills. Bringing his hands down from his mouth while he works to navigate the yolk down his dry throat without coughing, he places another small shell delicately into this spiral, moving two shells aside to keep everything in order.

Suddenly the door of the shack crashes open, and Egg is startled into crushing the tiny blue robin's egg he was holding. It's Red in the doorway, staring down at Egg's hand and the teardrop of yolk on his thumb.

"Egg, you fool!" he shouts. "Hey, you want some water? I mean, you got any water?"

"No," Egg says. "I can still suck plenty of life out of these."

"Your eggs are too black even for a 'coon to eat," Red sniffs. "And you're still nursing on these rotten things? Strongest stomach ever, I swear to Christ Almighty."

Red trails off as he walks to the one windowsill without an egg shell adornment. Instead, there's a row of wasps' heads staring up at him. Waiting for Red to figure out what he's looking at, Egg scratches at the letters of his nickname he's carved into a loose board on the crate.

"You still carving that everywhere," Red asks him over his shoulder, tapping at an insect's antenna. "Why are you carving that everywhere? I never really looked, but I always thought it was your name. But you're carving it with those dots atwixt the letters, like it's your initials. Is that possible? Are you the unluckiest bastard ever that your name is '**E.G.G.**'? Is your name 'Ernie'? Don't tell me I've been friends with an 'Edward Eggfucker Grabass' all this time."

Egg stops scratching, almost corrects him, says nothing. Red picks up a wasp head and pops it between his fingertips.

"Yeah, don't answer," he says. "I wasn't really asking. I'd really ask if I gave two shits." He wipes his hands and stares at Egg a while. Then, "Okay, I'll bite. What the holy hell is going on with these critters and their heads?"

"They keep me from getting stung. The heads watch over me. I haven't been stung since I lined them up like that."

"No, you haven't gotten stung since the last hornet died six months ago. Without water, your little friends were probably the first to go. Or the third, after various varmits. Well, okay, maybe the second to go. After Gray!"

Red circles Egg and swipes the shells off another windowsill with the side of his hand. Egg flinches, then flinches again when Red drops a whiskey bottle between Egg's legs and heads for the door.

"I don't even want to know what you're doing with all those shells. Chickens never stung me, and I don't need *that* voodoo." He laughs and tightens his hat. "You don't make no sense, Egg. Never will, I guess."

Egg figures he's on his way out and holds up another shell, lightly blowing on the tiny hole he's poked in one end.

"Answer me this though," Red says at the door. "How do you keep from breaking those when you're sucking on them?"

"You ever dealt with an 'eggbound' chicken?" Egg asks around puffs.

"Hearn it."

"Well, if a chicken gets an egg stuck, it'll go on making eggs and never layin' 'em, fillin' itself up with eggs until it bursts. You have to get that egg that's stuck up there or else that chicken will die. And you have to do this without breaking it."

"Why not just stick a finger up there and crush it?" Red asks.

"'Cause as soon as the egg explodes, just that fast, the chicken dies of shock. You have to take the end of the egg that's peeking out and put a tiny hole in it. Then you can gently crack the egg to pull it out, but only after you put your mouth down there and you slowly suck out what's—"

"Whoa!" Red yells. "No, no, no. Stop." He opens the door then turns around again. "So, Egg, if you were sucking on one of these in your mouth when someone punched you in the goddamn face, you think you might die of shock when it popped, too?"

Egg looks up at him startled, then almost smiles. This is something that he's never considered, but it sounds to Egg like a glorious end. Then Red walks out, and he's back to his blowing.

***

Bisbée. Same night.

Sam is walking along a dirt road, until his foot stumbles on the top of a wagon wheel mostly buried in the dirt. He adjusts his path at the wheel, and continues walking into a field until he's come up behind a slanted farmhouse. Kicking around some more, his boot rattles a horseshoe hidden in the brush, and he reaches down to reveal a trapdoor in the ground. It opens with a deep inhale of night air, and something scampers out of the hole and crunches off into the weeds near his feet. He frowns at this, wondering how something could be living in there, sealed up like a tomb all these years. Still, he doesn't hesitate very long. And with his own deep inhale, he steps down a rope ladder into the dark. The door slams shut after him with a crash.

An hour later, a coyote sniffs around the horseshoe but finds nothing of interest.

***

Agua Fría. Same night.

The Preacher slams his tattered chunk of Bible against his legs, and more pages fly off and flutter around him. The skin on his face is stretched tight against his skull, splitting bloody red rivers as he cackles, his eyes bugging out from dehydration. He's neck deep in another manic sermon. It's his fifth of the day.

"Don't worry about those pages, brother and sisters. That's how we weed out the shit we don't need."

He slams the Bible against his forehead, and another page comes loose. He catches this one before it hits the ground.

"Here, I'll prove it to you," he says, turning the page over to read and clearing his throat hard. The rattle in his neck sounds like a boot heel twisting in sand.

"'*If any man thirst, come to me and drink.*' Hmmm. Is that Jesus? I thought we got rid of the Jesus half when I tore the book down the middle! Okay, what else we got here..."

He shakes another page loose and holds it up to read.

"'*Do not have sexual relations with an animal and defile yourself with it. A woman must not present herself to an animal to have sexual relations with it. This is a perversion...*'" He throws the paper into the air. "Now, do we really need to read that to know it's true? Ain't that like sayin', 'Don't eat a bullet, kids, it might hurt'?"

He smacks the Book against his forehead again and grabs the next page that falls.

"'*Lust is the craving for salt for a man who is dying of thirst.*'"

The Preacher stands silent, pondering this quote a minute.

"Come on! What are the chances?" he laughs, then stops and looks around. "But no, I'm truly asking you. Is that really in there? I honestly don't remember that one at all."

He shakes off whatever disturbed him as he drops what's left of the Bible to his feet. Then he claps his hands in front of his face, covering his head in a cloud of dust and parchment.

"Okay! Where were we? We were talking about arrogance and anger, weren't we? Well, you know, one of those pages reminded me of something, my children. I lost my temper today, and here's how it happened. I got up early, chewed on a stick for breakfast, washed it down with a nice cup full of thorns, then walked out the door so fast I forgot to wear my white collar, the collar which has long since turned gray anyway. And 'cause people kinda look the same these days, I am no longer recognized without it! And one of you, someone out there right now, one of you came around a corner and saw me tearing some more pages out of the Book and asked me, appalled, if I was a Christian man, a God-fearing man. But that wasn't really what you were asking. Sure, those were the *words* you used, but what you were *really* asking me, what the words might not have revealed at first listen, was… if I had ever thought about fucking a dog."

Some worshippers gasp and turn to look at each other again. Two of them stand up and leave, appalled. The three remaining dried, dehydrated faces are utterly identical, not men or women anymore, asexual corpses, hollow eyes almost an inch deep into their skulls. They clasp hands and rock back and forth, hoping for some sort of reason to find its way back to their leader.

Robby Wendler peeks in from under a tent flap again, unnoticed this time. His face is healthy, clear-eyed, and amused. After surveying the scene, he adjusts the gun-shaped rock in his belt like a gunfighter and confidently crosses his arms, pretending to be a lawman with everything under control.

He runs when the Preacher's gaze turns his way, following the two others around the stick holding up the entrance.

"Hey, where's everyone going?" the Preacher shouts. "This will all make sense when I'm done, I swear! I'm sorry, did I swear? I meant 'I promise.' Whose boy was that anyhow?"

He looks to the sky.

"Sorry for the swearing, Lord. And you're prolly asking yourself, 'What does zig-zaggin' a canine have to do with being a Christian?' Precisely! I didn't make that connection! They did! Also, I saw someone eating a rotten apple today. An apple is halfway to wine, halfway to hell, but that's not why I told you not to do that. We'll come back to all that later..."

Someone in front scratches his head at that, and the fingers across the scalp makes sounds like a broken bottle on a boulder.

"Here's the point... the arrogance it takes to ask someone that question is incredible. If you see someone doing something you disapprove of, and you decide to ask them if they're a Christian, well, that's just too smug for words! As if that question has anything to do with the offense you're witnessing! As if you think that one question will get to the heart of everything they're doing, and everything they've done, for the duration of their entire life, leading up to this one moment, right now in front of you, this thing that offends you so much that you don't know a goddamn thing about! Well, you may as well be asking them if they ever fucked a dog. So watch what you ask me next time. Amen."

A moment of silence as the remaining worshippers frown and the wheels in their weary brains rattle almost audibly, trying to work out any kind of message in the madness. Finally, a hand is tentatively raised somewhere in the middle of the crowd.

"Yes, sir! I mean, ma'am! Damn, you're looking rough."

"Uh, do you mean fucking a dead dog?" a confused voice asks. "Or are you talking about a dog that's still alive?"

"Finally, a question worth answering! I'll get back to you on that after I find out."

***

Saloon. Same night.

Four drunk, dusty, dying men sit around a table, playing poker, four bottles of whiskey in front of them with only two full swigs left total. As one man slowly deals a hand, the cards begin to disintegrate in his fingers. No one seems to notice this. One man brings a lazy grip down on the dealer's arm to accuse him of cheating, and pieces of a crumbling ace of spades fall from the dealer's sleeve. The man across from him slowly stands up and pulls a knife. He throws it at the cheating dealer with little force, and the knife hits him in the face handle-first, then clatters harmlessly on the floor. After a moment, the knife thrower wearily sits back down and takes the last half-drink from his bottle.

They keep playing. And playing. The black dog that Little Joe pulled from the exodus of townspeople, only to kick away from his path when it followed him ten feet, now crawls around under the table of dying men, slowly weaving in and out of their legs, looking for something to scavenge. It navigates their limbs with snakelike movements until the smallest man at the table kicks at it in anger.

"You know, the only reason people abuse animals is so that they'll forget they're starving," Smallest Man says. "The animals, I mean."

"What?" Dealer asks.

"You truly believe this?" Knife Thrower asks.

"Who gives a shitfire," Smallest Man says, kicking out again right as the dog comes to life and lunges to knock him from his chair. Before anyone can react, the dog has ripped out the man's throat and is gorging itself on the blood, tendons, and neck jerky. The dealer stares for a moment and then spits at the dog's head. His saliva is heavy and black, and the dog flinches and gets lower, but keeps on feeding. Turning back to the game, the dealer tries to shuffle the cards and they fly apart into dust, and Knife Thrower shakes his head.

"Hey, I tried," Dealer shrugs.

"Where'd you get that tobacco?" Knife Thrower asks.

"I ain't chewing tobacco," Dealer says.

They play on and the dog chooses new throats at its leisure.

***

Bisbée. Edge of the edge of town. Dawn.

Tom rides his horse around a row of trees and comes to a clearing. In the middle of the field, The Ranger sits back in his saddle, arms crossed. The Ranger's nervous black Mustang snorts loudly and blows a cloud of snot into the air. Tom and his horse are startled by this, and Tom works to steady the animal.

"Whoa! Hey, Ranger! What are the chances of running into you out here?"

"What are you doing, Tom?" the Ranger asks, emotionless.

"My job, boss! So you can stop pouting and put that latchpan back in your mouth. You yourself sent us out with a list of faces and numbers, remember?"

"You have no business out here."

"What do you mean 'out here'? This ain't the moon. This ain't Hell. This is just another town. And out *there*, across that desert, that's just another town, too."

The Ranger turns to look to the horizon where Tom is pointing.

"I'm afraid you're wrong about a lot of things," he says. "That last thing you said, especially."

"Show me the wanted poster you kept for yourself, and I'll turn around right now."

The Ranger turns his horse in contempt and starts to ride away.

"You don't understand a goddamn thing."

Tom coaxes his horse to follow.

"That's fine," Tom says. "I don't understand a lot of things. Thank Christ for that."

"That's right. And it's too late to learn."

***

Agua Fría. Midday.

Red and his gang, Egg, Mud, Jackass, and Little Joe, are spread out under a dead tree where the shade would have been. They're all drunk or drinking, except for Red and Little Joe. Jackass drains a bottle and throws it. He pulls his gun to shoot the empty bottle but can't seem to muster the energy. He reholsters his weapon, pulls another bottle from a huge bag of whiskey bottles at his feet, and leans back against the tree trunk with a sigh.

"Anybody know any jokes?"

Egg scratches his head a minute, then reaches into a small sack and pulls out a spider as large as his hand. It's a Camel Spider, a large, desert dwelling creature that looks kind of like a hairy, urine-colored lobster. Jackass and Mud scramble to their feet to get far away from it.

"What the may hay is that?!" Mud hollers.

"Kill that fuckin' thing!"

Jackass slaps the spider out of Egg's hand, and Mud quickly stomps on it. Red and Little Joe move in for a closer look. For a second, everyone thinks the spider is dead. Then the spider stands up and starts walking toward Egg. Eyes full of relief, he picks it back up and pets it like a cat. Glaring up at Mud, Egg's hand hovers over his gun.

"Go, ahead, Egg," Mud taunts him. "Skin it."

They stare at each other.

"Go on, kill me over a fuckin' bug," Mud smiles. "One thing, if you don't kill me? You better look over your shoulder the rest of your life because one day I'm gonna be there and on that day..."

Red kicks Mud in the ass, sending him tumbling.

"Shut up," Red says. "How I ended up the box herder for you bitches is one great mystery." Then to Egg, "That thing really ain't dead? Okay, now I'm scared."

Egg relaxes and takes his hand away from his gun. Then he puts a protective arm around the spider.

"Don't no one try to kill it again," he says. "Not that you can. I tried stepping on it the first time I saw it following me. That's how we met. Me looking under my boot."

"Well, bugle on the bowl!" Red barks. "That's how I met your ma, too!"

Jackass comes over to squint.

"What the hell is it, Egg?"

"It's a Camel Spider. Heard all about them the one day I went to school. Did you know that these things can go a week without water? But only three days without food? That's the exact opposite of us."

"No, that's a 'camel,' yer thinking of, shitbird," Mud says from the ground. "Not a 'camel spider.' In fact, I doubt there's any such thing as a camel spider."

"Then what the hell is this?" Egg says, holding it up.

"That's what we're asking *you*, asshole!" Mud yells.

"Quit yaffin', I said that wrong before," Egg frowns. "It's not 'three days without food.' It's three days without biting someone! That's what it can't do."

"Just like Red over there," Jackass says. "He can't go one day without biting someone."

"I'm thinking there's a lot of other things it can't do, Egg," Red says, still fascinated. "Like write a letter, or wipe its ass. Not that it isn't amazing."

"You can't write a letter, you fuckin' lickfinger," Mud says, getting up.

"I can wipe my ass," Red says. He holds up a boot and wiggles it in the air. "Yours, too."

"Why couldn't it wipe its ass though?" Jackass asks. "It's got eight legs!"

"Shit!" Red laughs. "That means it's got four asses!"

"It's real smart," Egg pleads, holding it out in front of him. "Watch."

He walks away from the tree and puts the spider down in the dirt. He takes a few steps away from it and, in a flash, it runs to follow him. The gang is startled.

"Whoa!"

"It loves you, Egg! Just like us!"

Egg takes a few more steps and again the spider follows, stopping only when he stops.

"Maybe that thing does have a brain bigger than a bird," Jackass says.

"Bullshit," Little Joe says, coming in close to join in. "It's not following him. It's following his shadow. That's what those things do, they run and stop in your shade. That's why people are scared of them because they think it's chasing 'em. But all it wants is your shadow, to get outta the sun."

"I don't know," Red says. "Egg's so fuckin' skinny, it's hard to believe a bug could even fit in his shadow."

"And they ain't that hard to kill either," Little Joe says, hat brim up and stalking it.

"You saw it get stepped on and laugh it off," Jackass reminds him.

"Because it sees the shadow of your foot coming down and it rolls up in a ball," Little Joe says. "You just have to watch it real close. That's all it does."

Red claps his hands.

"Okay! Let's try something then."

Red walks over and shoves Egg to the ground. The spider crosses over to Red's shadow instead of Egg's and stops. Red takes a step and it takes a step with it. Red trots and the spider picks up speed. Red laughs and starts running and the spider scampers to catch up.

"All right," Red says, slowing down. "That's enough of that." He spits at the spider. "Back off!" Then he walks back toward the gang, the spider following.

"I said, back the hell off," he hisses at the spider again. Then he frowns and spits black tobacco juice at it again. It stops following, dipping a leg into the pool of brown spit, almost playing around.

Red starts walking slow, and the spider keeps pace again, always right in the center of Red's shadow. Then Red turns and pulls his gun, and Egg runs between Red and the spider, quickly picking it up off the ground.

"Don't do it, Red," Egg says, slow and serious, and Red seems genuinely surprised by his tone.

"You ever hear the phrase 'choose your battles'? Dumb fuckin' biscuit eater. You decide to stand up for the first time in your life over this nit? Why is that? There wasn't a fly around here you wanted to risk your life for instead? Maybe a rock that needs you to save it?"

They stare at each other in silence, and Little Joe walks over, diggin' in his pocket. He pulls out the leopard gecko from the magic trick at the Preacher's tent.

"Got an idea," Little Joe says. "Let's see if they'll fight."

Red's smile comes back fast.

"I'll go with that."

"Fine," Egg nods. "Put the lizard down."

They put the lizard and the spider down in the shade of the dead tree and stare awhile. Neither creature does anything.

"Just wait," Little Joe says. "Lizards will try to eat anything. Even if it's five times bigger than their head."

"Just like Egg!" Red laughs.

The gecko takes a lazy lunge at the spider and gets a leg in its mouth. Then it sits, unable to swallow any more. The spider doesn't even seem to notice the infraction. After a while, Little Joe reaches down to separate them.

"That was a great fight, boys," Red says, sarcastic. "Ain't seen that much action since yesterday on the toilet."

Little Joe slowly pulls the spider's leg from the gecko's mouth, and Egg quickly snatches the spider away from him to put it back in his bag. Little Joe holds the gecko up to Red's face.

"You ever look real close at this thing?" he asks him. "At its head? Why is there a hole in its head is what I want to know."

Red looks at the gecko's earholes, eyes narrowing, dark thoughts clouding his face.

"Those can't be ears, can they?" Little Joe asks. "Going all the way through its head like that?"

Red turns to look at his horse that's standing nearby. The gang's other horses root and snort through the brush around them, but Red's horse looks right at Red, its yellow eyes locked, no movement or sound from the animal except a slow, sick swaying. Then the horse's head catches just the right angle and flashes alight as a sunbeam cuts through the skull. The horse starts to wander off and the light through its head fades again.

"Hey! Where you think you're going!" Red yells. "Limsy, I'm talking to you, goddammit!"

Egg puts two fingers in his mouth and whistles loud. The horse's ears perk up and it quickly turns around.

"How the hell did you…" Red starts, shocked, the memory of something in the back of his eyes as the horse walks back, staring at him again. Red blinks hard, takes a deep breath, and noticing Little Joe next to him, angrily swats at him to get away, for everyone to stay away.

"I never could whistle like that," he says. "Only children can make noises like that."

And just like that, he's livid again.

"Everyone put your goddamn toys away."

"You got it, boss," Little Joe nods, pointing at everyone in turn. "Anyone seen my dog?" he asks, and Red gets scared, thinking they're still talking about spiders and the strange things they can do.

"There ain't no spiders! There ain't no dogs!" Red yells, running over to punch Little Joe square in the face. "There's nothing in this town but us!"

After three more punches, he convinces the rest of the gang that there was never a spider, or a lizard. Or a Little Joe either.

He's right about the spider.

NINE

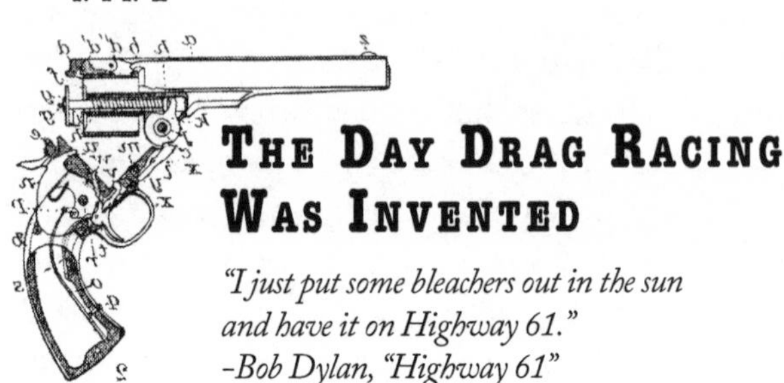

The Day Drag Racing Was Invented

"I just put some bleachers out in the sun
and have it on Highway 61."
-Bob Dylan, "Highway 61"

Desert. High Noonish and hot.

The Ranger and Tom are guiding their horses slowly and carefully through a long field of jagged, black rock. The horses' legs wobble alarmingly with each step, every sharp crack causing the men sit up straight in their saddles and hold their breath. After a long respite, the Ranger takes a moment to tug on his leather gauntlets and tighten his riding gloves. Imitating him, Tom pulls out a pink-and-turquoise beaded pair from his belt, ones he'd picked up at a Buffalo Bart Wild West show, the very worst of the Buffalo Bill knockoffs.

"What is it about every time we stop next with our animals neck and neck that I want to race your ass. These can openers on my boots practically start singing! We just need a signal. Give us a shot in the air, Ranger. Any signal will do."

The Ranger says nothing, just keeps messing with his gloves until he clicks his lips to get his horse moving again.

When they finally clear the rubble, Tom stops and dismounts. Toeing the dust and picking up a broken twig or two, he sniffs out a worn horse trail along their path that any fool could have noticed, but before he can point, they've spotted a caravan coming from the south.

They trot to intersect, but a hundred yards further on up, they catch sight of another long line of wagons and riders approaching from the southwest. Another three hundred yards or so, these three packs of travelers converge.

The Ranger looks them over as they cross projected paths, while Tom tips his hat at the men on point, trying for someone's attention, anyone in charge. Both caravans are on the edge of death, obvious refugees from Agua Fría, and they take no interest in the two men who have split the groups like Moses cutting through the Dead Sea. The dying riders slowly creep along, swollen tongues pushing on cracked lips, saliva hanging thick from the bridles of the horses. The Ranger waves Tom back to him, and they pull their horses to the side to watch the caravans cross. Lead riders for each group reveal themselves eventually, horses heading towards each other at a snail's pace. Amused, Tom shakes his head at the Ranger, who holds up a finger to keep him quiet. The two lead riders walk their dazed horses closer and closer, until their snouts actually rub together, metal and leather tangling them up, pulling each man to the side, almost to the group. The men stop, and the convoys behind them stop, and the two riders wearily look up from under their brims to notice each other as creatures sharing the planet.

"Where'd *you* come from, lubber?" ask the First Rider.

"What do you mean?" the Second Rider laughs. "Where'd you come from?"

"How could you not see me or my cavallard?" the First Rider goes on, adjusting his glasses, blood coming back into his face. "I've been moving in a straight line for 38 hours. How can a straight line be at fault in any equation?"

"You can't ride in a straight line forever, you crazy bastard," Second Rider says. "You'll eventually hit something. Unless that straight line is up."

"Or down," First Rider says, angry.

"What are you saying? Did you not see me? Do you still not see me now?"

Second Rider seems genuinely worried to hear the answer to this.

"What I'm saying is, if I never altered my path, then I'm not the one responsible for such a collision."

"I ain't moving."

"No, I am the straight line in this equation."

Tom can't help but bark a laugh at this exchange, but the Ranger chews on his lip, fighting the urge to join in. Despite the obvious fact that these men and their animals are teetering on the precipice of death and dehydration, or maybe because of it, the comedy of the moment is intoxicating.

"Listen up, men!" Tom shouts. "No one has to move. You're not even on a trail anymore. There's no reason you can't go around each other. Enough world left to make tracks in any direction."

The riders ignore Tom, and it takes him and the Ranger a fat minute to realize that the First Rider with the glasses is slowly pulling a gun from his belt. The other starts reaching for his gun, too, and Tom and the Ranger shake their heads as they watch what has to be the most lethargic quick draw in history. As the men continue to bring up their guns, arms straining with the weight of a thousand pounds, Tom holds up a pocket watch to show the Ranger, tapping the glass sarcastically. Faces red from the effort, the two riders' shaking hands work to steady their weapons as they continue to aim.

"Look at those two mockered motherfuckers. It's like watching men trying to hold horses over their heads!" Tom marvels. "Hey, Bob, should I time this bullshit? Anyone wanna slow-roast a pig while we wait!"

One of the guns finally fires, at least that's how the action appears to the men. A flash and smoke, and a rider's elbow bucks backward. But he hits nothing, no evidence of this shot going anywhere at all. Tom leans forward on his saddle, expecting it to drop from the end of the barrel like a loose tooth off a split lip. Then one of the riders slides off his horse and onto the ground, his body collapsing into itself like a rotten accordion. The default winner of the world's slowest gunfight reholsters his weapon and waves his people to follow him past the other caravan and the mirror images of their own cracked faces.

Tom holds up his canteen, ready to offer a sip to the victor. Within reason, of course. But he passes on by, the people, too, and they still take no notice of Tom or the Ranger, or anyone besides their leader. Then the now-orphaned caravan adjusts their course to follow the lead rider that remains, like ants on a scent trail back to their hole.

The march makes it a few steps into the valley of black rocks when the horse carrying the victor stumbles to its knees, carpus popped and swelling bigger by the second. The Ranger recognizes the crack, as loud as a black branch in the rain. The horse seems to deflate, but keeps stumbling forward, dumping the rider to the rubble in the process. The convoy trudges past where he lays unconscious or dead, and, now leaderless, they pick up their pace as they begin to scatter in all directions.

"Hey!" Tom yells at anyone. "What the hell is wrong with y'all?"

The Ranger stops him with a look.

"These people are too far gone," he says.

"Can't they even see where they're going? Could they be so moppy they couldn't see us? It's honest to God like they couldn't see us."

"Tom, in three more days, drunk or not, we won't even be able to see us either."

Tom and the Ranger both lean back to watch the remainder of the two convoys trample into the black rocks. As they file past, the condition of the refugees gets worse and worse, like months passing before their eyes. In the middle of the line, around the groups still guarding wagons and other belongings, some of the people are slumped across the backs of their horses, any faces still visible grinning like drum skins stretched across skulls. But the longer the line goes, the more backwards and primal the people seem to get. Further down, two children are fighting over half of something dead. Further past that fight, wild-eyed men are struggling to eat something that's still alive. Further past them, a wild-eyed woman is devouring something thick and pink that she won't let anyone see, an expression of pure pleasure on her face, as if she can't believe the miracle sustenance she's discovered, a tiny blue bonnet hangs from her red chin like a bib. And when the tail end of the caravan finally passes by, all the people slumped forward on these horses are clearly dead, long past dead really and now something else, like a wind-up army of corpses that keeps pace with the rest nonetheless. The Ranger turns away, instead watching more horses pile up in the distance as brittle bones snap on the field of black at the front of the line. He finally motions for Tom to follow as they leave the dead and the mad behind them.

***

Agua Fría. Edge of town. Dusk.

Red and his gang fidget around a campfire. Outlines of houses are visible a few hundred feet away. Three of the houses are burning.

"Why are we still sleeping outside?" Little Joe wants to know. "Look at all those empty stores, all those farms. We got the pick of the litter, boss!"

Red ignores him. He's still thinking about the spider, although he's forbidden the rest to mention it.

"It had me honey-fuggled at first, but I'll bet it's really easy to stomp on that bugger at night," he says. "It can't see any shadow at night, can it, Egg? Answer that and I'll kill you."

Egg says nothing, pulling his feet in closer to his body.

"Little Joe's right, boss," Mud says. "Why are we out here right now?"

"Listen up, Miss Nancy, you, too, Molly," Red says. "If we go sleep in some nice big bed, how we gonna pretend that we're stealing all their shit in the morning? It'd be like we were stealing from ourselves."

The gang glances at each other in confusion. Red kicks at the fire and it flashes a little higher.

"Anybody know any stories?"

Jackass takes a long drink and passes the bottle to Mud.

"Got an idea," Mud says, taking a swig. "Now that this town is ours, what's something you always wanted to do?"

"Good question, boys," Red says, happy again. "Back when you didn't have the balls to go through with it, what were some things you wished you woulda done?"

"I always wanted to 'desecate' in the middle of a church," Jackass says, wistful. "But it burned down."

"Hey, I wanted to shit in the church, too!" Mud says. "But you know what? I saw that crazy converter shitting there himself. Earlier today. Right in a pile of ashes where the pulpit used to be. He started to tell me why what he was doing wasn't blasphemous, and goddamn if I wasn't halfway convinced by the time he was done talking. But I had to walk away 'cause I just can't talk to someone while they're doing that."

"Shittin' you say?" Red frowns. "Shittin' means eatin'. Where's he getting food?"

"Hell, the only food he's getting is from a bottle," Mud says, getting up to walk over to Egg. He taps his own bottle against Egg's head to get his attention. Egg looks up slowly, eyes lost in thought. He takes the bottle from him even slower, pulling such a minuscule draw that Red kicks some dirt his way, frustrated with him as usual.

"Hey! What's your problem?"

"It's like we're ghosts, ain't it?" Egg says, licking the liquor from his lips. "Like we've been deceased since the bell rang."

Red savagely kicks more dirt, then more, kicking all the way up into Egg's face.

"Shut that shit up," he says with one last kick. There's a rock in that splash of dirt, and Egg's eyes flash in anger for a moment when it clips his chin. Then he takes a bigger drink from the bottle and clears his throat.

"Okay, you want to know?" he says, taking another swig. "Here's something I always wanted to do. You know those eggs I collect?"

"No, what eggs, *Egg*?" Red mocks.

"The ones you're always sucking on?" Mud snickers, and Jackass holds up a hand.

"You know what?" he says. "Those rotten eggs will probably help him last a day longer than us. At least an hour. He might be stronger than he looks."

"Well, I keep the shells," Egg continues. "I keep 'em all. Keep 'em intact, keep them whole. Then I take about fifty or so scorpions, and I milk the venom from their tails."

The men stop harassing him to listen more closely. Red crosses his arms.

"Then I fill up these eggs—Robin's eggs are the perfect size, but around here you get mostly catbirds and bushtits—and then I carefully hold one egg unbroken in the back of my mouth." Egg pauses, excited with all the suspense he's building. "But, wait! Earlier in the day, I'll have picked out someone, someone that made me mad. And I'll find a way to cut their hand, just a little cut, acting like it's an accident. Maybe rig a bottle to explode while they're squeezing it, maybe by handing them a knife the wrong way, maybe by hanging enough mirrors that they finally try to punch themselves in the face."

Red uncrosses his arms.

"Then I try to make a deal with that man, or apologize, or something, come up with some reason for him to shake my hand and seal that deal by us spitting in our palms. That's when I crack the egg in my mouth, spit on my hand, and shake his paw as hard as I fucking can."

Then Egg holds up a hand like he's daring someone to shake it.

"Scorpion honey don't always kill," Red says after a second, half smiling but not moving for the hand. "In fact, I don't think they ever kill."

"Doesn't matter," Egg says, hitting the bottle again. "All you have to do is tell them what you did, or what you could do, and their brains will do all the rest. And if my handshake doesn't kill them, it'll slow them down enough to where something else could get the drop on them." His fingers drum the bottle. "Ain't nobody want to try me, chickenshits?" he asks, sweetly.

The bottle explodes in Egg's hands, showering everyone with

whiskey, glass, and blood. Egg curls up to stop his fingers from bleeding while Red laughs and reholsters his smoking gun.

"Quit thinking so hard," he says. "You don't need all that plannin'. Don't need to rig no bottle to explode. Dry as we are, everyone around here cuts their hands a hundred times a day just waving hello."

"Hello!" Mud waves from somewhere in the dark.

***

Bisbée. Forty years ago. Weather unpredictable.

Back in the gun store. Little Bobby Ford, a Future Arizona Ranger, and his father, Sam, are still working their way through a special kind of calendar, consisting of a dozen weapons laid out on the counter. The Future Ranger's hand is too small for every pistol he tries, but Sam has high hopes for a particularly ornate shooter.

"This is April's gun," Sam says. "Very appropriate for 'April,' since it's a woman's name. Woman's shooter, too, probably. It's the .38 Single Action, decorated in silver and gold by Tiffany & Company. Polished to perfection. It was actually presented to General George Custer in 1869. It looks like it's made from cake icing because it's the most expensive gun in the case. But no one has *ever* thought about stealing it because they don't want the firearm that proved once and for all that Custer *was* a homosexual. You know what that is? On second thought, don't even touch it, boy."

They start to move down, but Sam stops and goes back.

"You know what this gun looks like to me?" he asks his son. "It does look like the kind of gun a girl would carry... if it was the kind of girl who *wouldn't* normally carry a gun, get me?"

They move down to a long rifle which Sam quickly picks up. To the Future Ranger's surprise, Sam breaks it in half over his knee.

"May," he says. "The Smith & Wesson Revolving Rifle. It looks like a rifle, but it's really just a revolver with a long, detachable barrel and shoulder stock. Developed in 1875, this particular gun saved its owner's life when he pretended to fall and smash his very own weapon. Then, when his attackers' backs were turned, in five seconds tops he put it back together and shot them all down. Shot them in the back you ask? No, of course not. You should never shoot someone in the back. He shot them in the back of their goddamn *heads*. And May is a good time to use this rifle, too. Lots of turkeys to shoot. And it's good sport to hone your talents because the back of a turkey's skull is real tiny."

Sam snaps the rifle back together and pushes his son past it to the next one.

"June's gun. This is the weapon built after both Horace Smith and Daniel B. Wesson survived their first gunfight. It's the S&W Model 1. Fired a tiny .22 Rimfire short cartridge—"

"They had a gun fight?" the Future Ranger interrupts. "Against each other? Did that really happen?"

His father ignores the question and moves down again.

"July. This is the .38 Super built to compete with the Colt .45 and the .38 Colt Super Automatic. I'm not a Colt fan, but they say that Smith & Wesson are still, to this day, obsessed with topping this gun. They say that they're working on something called a 'Magnum' as we speak, whatever the hell that is. Sounds like a goddamn Indian name to me. Goddamn thing must shoot arrows and sadness. We'll see."

They move down again, then both stop to stare at a small, thin gun that resembles a child's toy.

"I fuck with this weapon every August," Sam says. "Built in 1887 and used in the 1908 Olympics, Smith & Wesson built this Target Revolver with the first adjustable site. They stopped building them because the 1908 Olympics were such a fucking joke with rich, weak bastards having slap-fights and staring contests and other equally stupid shit. Did you know that the rules in the first Olympics were designed to keep real athletes from competing? Smith pulled this gun from the exhibition and publicly said they were embarrassed to be a part of it. Rumor has it that he did this after he saw an Apache laughing his ass off at the thumb-wrestling contest. Yes, son, the Apaches *did* invent thumb-wrestling, but their version is to the death. Or maybe that was 'Sue' Indians. Anyhow, I set up a little target practice of my own every August, when it's the hottest part of the year. Ever try to shoot the thumb off an eagle? They're the only animal besides us that's got thumbs, you know."

"True story?"

"True story."

Sam picks up the next gun in the line, holding it over his head to show his son a long, metal chain dangling off of the grip.

"September. Built in 1861, this here's the Model 4 American. Actually it's a variation on the Model 2. But it turned out to be just too goddamn big. The extractor rod is attached with a chain only slightly longer than a bulldog's leash. In fact, that's what people used this damn chain for. Instead of throwing a stick, they'd throw the extractor rod, and the dog would bring it back. It was a good way to teach the dog to bring back the ducks you shot with it. Also makes a good splint."

Then they finally come to a small lump of a revolver so dull and dirt-covered that it's almost invisible. It seems to be made of rock or maybe carved from a chunk of dead wood as a joke. The Future Ranger reaches for it excitedly, his small hand covering the grip perfectly.

"Paw, what year is it, right now, I mean?"

"Why?"

"The years on these guns, the months. The math is hurtin' my head."

"They're gonna hurt more than that in a second if you don't pay attention."

"But I am. That's the problem."

His dad's grip smothers his son's hand, and when they both squeeze the gun together, the metal is so cold that the boy's teeth start clicking, and little Bobby, the future Arizona Ranger, thinks his father has turned it to September just by speaking the word.

TEN

One That Sunk

"Hey, little girl, is your daddy home?
Did he go and leave you all alone?"
-Bruce Springsteen, "I'm On Fire"

Agua Fría. Morning. Today.

The Ranger and Tom are entering the city limits. Their first glimpse of the town is such an obscene vision of hell that it's almost comical, particularly to Tom, who has maintained his sense of humor throughout many atrocities. A broken signpost marks the border, as does a blazing bonfire of dead horses. A line of silent storefronts loom in the distance like tombstones, vultures perched on their rooftops. As the Ranger and Tom approach the fire of horseflesh and bone, Tom chuckles and points at the animals' legs protruding from the flames. The Ranger stops his horse, and Tom does the same, then clears his throat and points some more.

"You know what," Tom says. "I once rode into a town, and the first thing I saw was this giant butterfly made out of a dozen kinda flowers. All the children there had built it just to welcome us. Turned out that my stay in that town was perfect, no fights, no sheriff, didn't lose no money. Then, this other time, years later, I rode into a different town, and some little bastard hit me with a ball of fecal from the roof of the bank. And my stay there only got worse after that."

"What's your point?"

"Point is, I'm thinking there's good omens, and there's bad omens. And I look at a fuckin' bonfire of horses and, uh, I ain't a superstitious man or anything but..."

As they circle the fire, the Ranger struggles to stop his nervous horse when he sees a man lying on the ground nearby, his arms behind his head and his hat covering his face. The man seems to be relaxing, and as they get closer, they see the hat move as if the man's snoring or breathing hard underneath it. The Ranger dismounts and walks closer. When he walks in front of it, his black Mustang blows a stream of mucus onto the Ranger's hat.

"Do you think there's a solitary horse left alive around here?" Tom asks him. Then, "Does that Mustang of yours got some kind of infection or what? We gotta be careful."

Tom trails off as the Ranger pulls back the hat to reveal the face of the cowboy on the ground. There's a boiling mass of maggots in the holes where his eyes, nose, and mouth should be. Tom stops laughing for good and coughs to stifle a gag. The Ranger starts unloading the gear off his horse.

"I ain't seen any flies in days. Or rain. Good thing I didn't pack my fish!" Tom jokes, still horrified and hacking up some smoke. "Tell me now, how the hell can there be maggots without flies?"

The Ranger ignores this observation, and the follow-up question.

"We'll camp here," he says, and Tom looks at him in shock for a moment, then dismounts and begins unloading his horse, too.

"Why not."

***

Agua Fría. Twilight.

Jackass walks up the steps of a porch of a house, eye on the lamp burning in the window. He's carrying an empty bucket in his hand. He peers into the one glowing window, then a couple dark ones, then he raps on the door. He hears something like a dog whimpering inside and puts his ear to the wood. After a couple seconds of silence, he hears the sound of growling and reaches for his gun. Cautiously, Jackass tries the doorknob.

"Hey, little girl," he says, then corrects himself. "I mean, little boy?"

There's another ominous growl, and the door quickly swings open inward on its own, the doorknob yanked from his hands. The shadow of a boy stands in the vestibule.

"Hey, son! What are you still doing here? Where's your family? You got any food or drink?"

The shadow says nothing. Jackass leans his head in to look around. The house is deserted except for the child. He laughs.

"Sorry, I thought you were a girl when I first walked up. Or a wolf. You know, little kids like you, you're too little to tell if you're a boy, girl, animal, or vegetable here in the dark. You ain't no vegetable are you!" Jackass steps inside and tries to sound authoritative. "I'm looking for water, boy. You got any water in there? Where's your ma or pa?"

"Maw? Or paw?" the boy asks back, stressing the W's. He's still hiding in the dark, and Jackass can hear the smile in his voice, but he misses the double meaning of the words.

"Yeah, you ain't got none?"

"They're gone."

"Oh. I see." Jackass starts to take another step but hesitates, suddenly nervous. "You sure you're alone in there, son? No cunne 'round hidin'?"

"Yep. Just me. No maw or paw."

Jackass almost gets it that time.

"You got any water in there? Vegetables like us need water, you know? You do, too, right?"

"Yes. Of course I do. Everybody does."

"What did you say?" Jackass is suspicious. "Everybody who? From where? Who else is in there with you, kid?"

"From where who what?" the boy asks back. "Water is from the wells. Always water in the wells."

Jackass looks in past the boy again, ready to ransack the place, but something about the boy is making him uneasy, making him wish his bottle was back in his mouth. In his drunken haze, he sees a boy in the shadow, then a girl, then, just for a flash, the shadow of a slumped animal. He jumps backs up a step. Then another, and suddenly he's back outside. The boy comes to the door.

"It's not our age that makes it so hard," the boys says. "And it's not the dark. It's only because you're thirsty that it's hard telling children apart."

"What?" Jackass scratches his head and backs up some more. In his stupor, he could have swore he heard the boy say something about "tearing children apart."

"You mean, 'cause *you're* thirsty, right?" Jackass says. Then, after a breath. "Who are you?"

The boy says nothing and Jackass sees the hints of a toothy smile in the shadows. Then light hits some incisors just right, and Jackass blinks at white teeth, impossibly healthy and strong. He heads back down the steps.

"I'll come back to check that well later!" Jackass says as he hits the dirt, stumbles, then trots away from the house. He hears the boy's voice echoing behind him.

"They lied to you about this town," the boy says. "There's always something to drink here."

***

Agua Fría. Edge of town. Dark.

The Ranger and Tom crouch next to the blazing horses all cavalier, like it's any other bonfire. Tom is playing his harmonica and staring at the legs in the flames.

"If this isn't a good time to blow some spooky notes on a harp, I just don't know what is," he says between lazy puffs of music. "Got anything I can quirley with this tobacco?"

"Nope," the Ranger grunts. Then he ponders, "You know, if someone dragged these horses over to burn them. Then that means there's people still here to worry about the stink."

Tom reaches into the fire and breaks off a horse's leg. Then he pulls strips of hide from the smoking limb as the Ranger gives him a curious stare. Tom stops skinning the leg and throws it back into the flames.

"Just a thought," he shrugs. "A charred horse hoof or a lathy bit of leg might look like a sweet, ripe peach to us in about 24 hours."

"How much water you got left?"

"Most of it," Tom says, patting his canteen and the bags near him. "Some jerky, too. But we have to finish our business tomorrow and ride straight the fuck out if we want to make it back."

The Ranger stands up and slaps some dirt off his legs.

"We will," he says. "If we don't waste time here telling stories."

"Ain't that what a campfire's for!" Tom says, punctuating this with some tuneless metal bleats.

"Not at all," the Ranger says. "A fire's something you stare at when you want to forget a story, not remember one."

"Whatever you say."

"Grab your squaw wood. We're on the move."

"Not till you tell me a bedtime story!" Tom says as he reluctantly packs up.

The Ranger stares at him for a solid minute.

"Okay, here's a five-second fable for you," he says. "When I was young, my father rigged every gun he owned, every gun in his shop, to explode when it fired. For some reason, he thought this was a good thing to do. Thought it would make me a man."

Tom considers this a moment.

"That ain't no fable," he decides. "A fable has a point."

"So does your fuckin' head."

There's a rustling and crackling of something moving in the brush behind them, and they both spin around quick, hands on their guns. They see the shadow of a boy disappear into the dark. The men exchange a surprised look, quickly finish loading up their horses, and swing legs up into their saddles to follow. The Ranger kicks his steed hard to get it moving.

"You should lighten up on the beast," Tom says. "Might do wonders."

"Have you ever noticed that everything bad that's happened to a man on a horse, happened to a man on a horse?"

Tom stares until he's satisfied the Ranger's question is serious.

"Forget it."

***

Five mile away, Jackass crouches down in an outhouse, head buried in the toilet, looking for signs of water, testing how strong his thirst has grown. His head comes up, gagging, coughing and dry heaving as he tumbles out, his empty bucket swinging and banging bruises against his legs. A mile later, he finds another outhouse in a field, and he opens the door, sucking in his breath to hold it again.

He's startled to see a man staring back at him.

In a flash, he drops the bucket, draws his gun and fires. Dead already, a chunk of the man's skull is blown up to streak the ceiling like war paint, and what's left of his forehead and brain rolls a lap or two around his neck and shoulders. Jackass lowers his gun, his aiming eye slowly opening as he waits to see if the man will fall to the side and give up his seat. He counts to three, still holding his breath, then hears a distinct *plop!* as the corpse defecates one last time. Jackass snickers as this somehow reminds him of his humanity. Then he closes the door and leaves.

Then he's back in a flash with his head wriggling like a vulture for the hole between the dead man's legs. His tongue hits the salt of blood and shit before the door stops swinging, and it's wonderful. He almost believed in God all over again as he fills his bucket to the brim before the last wet pieces of the dead man can sink.

***

A mile away, the Ranger and Tom ride down a dark dirt road toward the center of town. Silent storefronts, saloons, and shops loom, broken windows on all. A sign can barely be read by the light of the moon.

"Welcome to Agua Fria! Population: 672 + 1 - 663 - 3 x 13 flies – 1 dog – 27 chipmunks – 5 vultures – 2 frogs – 1 hog – 8 snakes – 13,000 locusts – 16 owls – 3 gators – 1 puma – 9 'coons – 6 coyotes – all the horses + 1 horse - 1 sheriff + 1 lizard = 9"

"It's like the worst Ark of all time! Maybe it's Noah's brother's, you know, the boat that sunk. You don't hear much about his family. Imagine all that zoonin'. Make yer ears bleed."

Out of the corner of his eye, the Ranger sees someone ducking behind a row of trees, and he slows his horse. It's Egg, squatting down to make himself small, furiously carving something into the trunk. Even though Egg is far away, the Ranger and him lock eyes for a long moment, and a flash of recognition passes between them. Then Egg stands up and pushes on the tree in front of him. The Ranger blinks as the thick trunk creaks and leans as if it's moments from falling over with ease.

"What the hell?"

Then Egg is up and running deep into the trees and gone. The Ranger catches a quick glimpse of a young boy running close behind Egg, then the boy is gone, too. The tree Egg pushed sways and crackles a bit more, then is straight and still. Tom looks toward the motion, but he's too slow.

"What? What did you see?" he asks.

"Up there. Past the trees. I thought..." the Ranger says, scratching his head under his brim. "Nothing. Forget it."

"Here's my question," Tom says. "Those trees over there. How do they stay alive in the middle of the desert. Or here, a town with no water?"

"Who says they're alive?"

"Well, they're still standing, ain't they?"

"Sometimes, if you die standing up, you can keep standing forever, Tom."

"No, something will always knock you down. And who says there's no water, by the way?"

They ride on in silence. Further down the road, another flutter of peripheral movement catches their eyes, and they turn their horses to watch a young boy run up the stone porch and into the front door of a nearby farm house. The Ranger suddenly stops his horse with a yank.

"I saw that one!" Tom yells. "You see that kid? He went right up into that damn house."

"I saw."

"You saw, huh. Well, what the hell's going on around here? I thought this town was dry. Do you know who lives there?"

The Ranger looks at him like he's debating if he'll answer.

"Yeah. I did before."

Then the Ranger spurs his horse and starts it trotting toward the farm in the distance.

"And this is the first time in my life I'm hoping she won't be home."

***

Bisbée. Thirty-some years ago, give or take a decade.

The gun store is ragged but still standing, just like Samuel, and a teenage Bobby Ford, future Arizona Ranger, is arguing with his father like it's his first time.

"Goddamnit, boy. He is too fast."

"So am I," the Future Ranger says.

"He's faster than most. Faster than you for certain."

"How did you know this?"

Sam throws a bottle against the wall closest to his son.

"Because I caught him playing with himself when he was eight!" he says.

"Blarney."

"I swear, son," Sam says. "Listen to me. He was eight years old, and his hand was moving so fast it looked like a hornet trapped under a shot glass. His mother actually talked a doctor into tying his right hand to his side for weeks. And, of course, what a mistake that was, 'cause when that hand finally broke free from those belts and ropes and knots, his jerkin'-off hand was three times faster than it was before. Guess which one he fires with."

"You're so full of shit," the Future Ranger says, trying not to smile.

"I ain't lying. That's the real reason Red left town. He hasn't seen his mother or been back to Bisbée since the day he untied his shootin' hand."

"Bull. Shit," the Future Ranger says, turning toward the door.

Sam grabs for his son's arm to keep him still, but he yanks it away and keeps walking.

"Hey, this ain't no joke, boy! If it's a gunfight... you're gonna die today."

The young Ranger stomps out the door in disgust. Sam watches him go, brow furrowed.

"Thanks for believing in me, daddy."

***

Bisbée. Still thirty-some years ago, but later that day, with a loaded gun.

A five-year-old boy is sitting on a branch in a lone tree on a hill. He folds a pocket knife and puts it into his pocket. Under him, a long road stretches off into the distance in two directions. At the vanishing point on the horizon, at both ends of this road, two young men on horseback are riding towards each other and the tree. As they ride closer to the boy on the branch, it becomes clear that it is a young Ranger and a very young Red riding up to meet. When they're about a hundred yards apart, the two go for their pistols.

Both draws are equally fast, but the Ranger's gun explodes in his hand.

Because of this, Red doesn't fire at all, laughing long and hard instead. Then, without a recognizable word, Red turns his horse around and rides away. The young Ranger slumps in his saddle, head down, then slowly looks up at a boy high in the trees. Their eyes meet. Then the Ranger turns his horse to ride off in the direction he came, cradling a curled, bloody hand against his chest.

This boy watches him go, climbing higher into the tangle of leaves. At the top where the branches are almost too thin to hold him, he reaches into a bird's nest and carefully removes the single egg tucked inside. As he's looking at the egg in his hand, the branch he's on suddenly snaps and dumps him hard onto the ground. He sits up, staring at his hand, a look of horror on his face. In his palm are shards of the shell, a swirl of blood and yolk, and a half-formed embryo. The boy throws it all as hard as he can and runs away.

ELEVEN

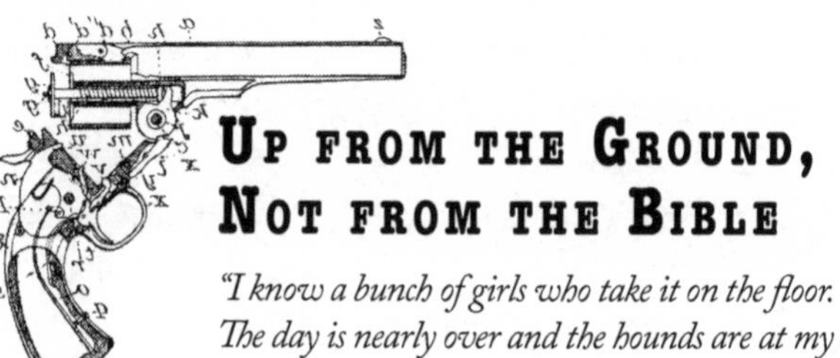

Up from the Ground, Not from the Bible

"I know a bunch of girls who take it on the floor.
The day is nearly over and the hounds are at my door."
-Sons of Maxwell, "Fox on the Run"

Agua Fría. Here and now. Night.

The Ranger and McKenna Wendler are walking through a dead cornfield. The stalks and leaves bend and bust into paper and dust across their shins as they march. They crunch along a good hundred yards without speaking, until they come to a dry-roasted riverbed at the edge of the field.

"I never thought I'd see you again," McKenna says.

"Me neither."

"So why did you come back? Pa send you?"

"You know why I'm back here."

"I don't know why you're back here, Bob. I don't know why you think I'd ever leave here, certainly not to see our father."

"Normally, I'd agree with you. But for the first time I think this town has become less desirable than our childhood home."

"Says you."

They step down into the dead riverbed and walk a little longer, stopping at a small puddle of water in the lowest part of the ditch. The Ranger is the first to notice this evidence of water, and he watches for McKenna's reaction. But she seemingly takes no notice, almost stepping in the mud before the Ranger puts an arm out to stop her. She looks up, alarmed.

"Hold on, McKenna. You need to answer this question for me. There's water in this town, ain't there?"

She looks straight ahead, saying nothing.

"Something else is going on here," he continues. "You wouldn't risk staying, risk your own son, unless something was going on. You have a good water source, don't you? At the very least, you got a stash. Tell me!" He turns her to face him.

"Even if you're right," she says. "We'd still be trapped."

"Why? Why can't you go now? Right now? Come back with us."

McKenna doesn't answer this and crouches down next to the small puddle.

"You have horses in your barn, don't you?" he says. "I thought I heard horses out there earlier."

She remains silent, and the Ranger kneels down next to her. There's a tiny, red fish swimming in circles in the puddle, looking for a way out, not understanding its predicament or the relative safety of its prison. The Ranger tips his hat up to get a closer look.

"You see that?" he asks her.

"Yes. I see it."

"Now how the hell did that fish get in there? Fish still can't walk, right? Wait, do fish walk around here? Keep in mind that no answer you can give will surprise me."

"The fish didn't go anywhere, Bob," she says with a weary smile. "And this one didn't come from anywhere either. It's always been right there. It's just everything around it that has changed. Just like this town."

The Ranger stands up quickly, her answer making him remember his mission.

"I'm sorry, but we're leaving here tomorrow. First light. We should be gone already."

He helps her step out of the ditch, and they turn back toward her house, walking on in silence a while longer. McKenna hums a folksong he first heard belted out by his drunk uncle Ron. The Ranger was certain it was sung while he was christened as a baby, but his father refused to verify the rumor. In his head, he fills in the words to her humming.

"She walks through the corn leading down by the river, her hair shone like gold in the hot summer sun..."

"Bob, did you stop to see your father on the way here?"

"Your father."

"Whoever."

"Yep, I sure did."

"Did you see our Uncle Ron?"

He thinks, "nope," but doesn't say it. She points to the pistol on his hip.

"Well, if you were at your dad's gun store, why didn't you get yourself another one?"

"You recognize her, huh?" the Ranger laughs, tapping his gun with a thumb.

"'Course I do. And it's still weird to call it 'her.' Don't men do that with boats, not guns?"

"Probably. Never had need for a boat."

"Never had need for a gun either. Didn't that gun almost kill you? Didn't your own father—"

"Stop calling him that," he interrupts. "Listen to me now. It wouldn't have mattered which gun I would have picked out of that case. He had taken a part or a spring or a pin out of every single weapon in his shop to make sure I would never kill no one. Taken 'em apart and put 'em back together wrong. And those histories! No way them manufacturin' years matched neither."

"At least he bothered to lie to you about such things."

"Ridiculous. At least I know what happens with this gun. A backfire is harmless enough, in the scheme of things. If I switched it with something else from his case, hell, something worse might happen. Probably get a gun that shoots backwards."

"But that doesn't make any sense, Bob. Why would our father risk your life and make sure you could never shoot back?"

"He thought it would make me tough, I guess," he says. "Force me to fight instead of shoot? I don't know. He reckoned those two things had a different result, as if every lambasting didn't usually end up on the ground, with thumbs fish-hooking mouths and eyeballs, men killing men or varmits with anything they can grab. He thought a different outcome, one without a bullet involved, would make a man outta me."

"Well, it sounds like that monster convinced you. And you must think he was right... if you're still carrying a broken gun," she says, picking up the pace of their walk as they clear the last of the crackling husks. "What did your father name it again? It *was* a girl's name, wasn't it?"

The Ranger laughs hard at the memory.

"Yeah, she was. And it was hard enough to grow up with a broken gun."

McKenna finishes his sentence, laughing with him.

"But it was even harder growing up with a gun named 'Sue.'"

They walk some more, house looming, and the Ranger pulls his hat back down, all business again, brain working out the details of their leaving.

"'Kenna, what happened to Gray?" he asks her.

She starts to speak, hesitates, then Robby runs up from the barn, and she drops her head. Robby skids to a stop in front of them, out of breath, eyes full of bad ideas. The Ranger's seen his look before.

"You must be Robert," the Ranger says. "How do you do, son. I'm your..."

"Come here right now, Robby," McKenna says, cutting him off.

Robby doesn't answer, and instead takes a protective step towards his mother and studies the Ranger up and down. McKenna reaches down and straightens the boy's huge flannel shirt.

"When are you gonna start wearing your own clothes?" she asks her son. "You realize that his shirts are going nowhere? You realize they'll be waiting for you to grow into them?"

"Hey, boy," the Ranger says. "You want to see something?"

The Ranger turns around and heads back for the ditch, and Robby comes out from behind his mother's legs to follow, staying a cautious distance behind. The Ranger stops at the small mud puddle and squats next to it.

"Look there."

"Huh? I don't see... wow!"

Robby drops to the dirt to get a better look at the tiny red fish darting around in the circle. He excitedly pokes at it, chasing it through the puddle with his finger. Then he stands up, eyes wide, and points further down the riverbed.

"*You* want to see something?" Robby says, then he runs about fifty feet down the ditch to wait impatiently for the Ranger. McKenna watches all of this from a distance, hands on her hips. When the Ranger catches up, he finds Robby standing proudly over a head-sized hole in the ground, and he laughs.

"Boy, when you say you're gonna show someone something, you don't show them the hole the 'something' was in instead."

"No. Look!"

Robby reaches into the hole and pulls out a rock.

"That's a nice rock, son. You find that out here, huh? Why don't you find us some music roots so your ma can mash 'em and we can eat sometime this century."

"I didn't find it out here. And I ain't saying where I found it, in case there's more. I just hide it there. What do you think?"

The Ranger tips up his hat again and squints at the rock in Robby's hand, not sure what kind of reaction the boy is waiting for.

"So, what do you got here... it looks... like a dog, right?"

"No! It looks like a gun!"

"Hey, you're right," the Ranger says, looking closer. "In fact, that looks so much like a gun, that might'a really been a gun a hundred years ago."

"There weren't no guns a hundred years ago," Robby frowns.

"How do you know? They could have all turned into rocks. Like that. Like this..."

The Ranger pulls his gray gun from its holster and holds it up in the sun. Then he holds it next to Robby's rock. McKenna walks up, looking frustrated, hands still on her hips.

"Hard to tell them apart, ain't it?" the Ranger says. "Now, ask your ma if there were people a hundred years ago."

Robby turns to his mother and asks, "Ma, were there people a hundred years ago?"

"Of course," she sighs.

"Then there were guns," the Ranger nods, reholstering his weapon.

"But there weren't no guns in the Bible," Robby says. "Preacher told me so."

"So what? There weren't no dinosaurs in there either."

"I know that," Robby says, frustrated. Then he drops his rock back into his hole and kicks a thin layer of dirt over it.

"Well, son. How do you know there weren't no guns in the Bible?" the Ranger asks. "They spoke another language back then. Who knows what they called it. The Lord may have been a crack shot."

Robby scratches his head.

"Tell you what," the Ranger says. "If there's guns in the Bible, and I'm right, I'll give you the mud pipes right off my feet. Hell, I'll trade you that special rock of yours for a real gun, for my gun."

Alarmed, McKenna grabs his arm, and the Ranger gives her a reassuring look, shaking his head like there's nothing to worry about.

"Ma? Is today Sunday?"

"I don't know anymore."

Satisfied with that answer, Robby climbs out of the riverbed and runs off, and McKenna starts after him.

"Robby!" she yells. "Don't let me catch you mousing around that church again, and don't you dare go to town. Wait!"

The Ranger takes her elbow and spins her around.

"Don't worry," he says to her. "Ain't no guns in the Bible. Ain't no church anymore either." Then he yells after her son. "Hey, boy. Hey, boy!"

The Ranger reaches into a pocket and retrieves what appears to Robby to be the boy's rock. He throws it towards Robby, who's now running straight back, terrified the Ranger stole his treasure. Out of breath, Robby picks it up and makes sure it's the right rock.

He turns it and turns it, unable to be sure.

"If it's a weapon, son," he says. "It always goes in your belt. Never lose sight of it again."

Robby pulls up his shirt tail and pushes the rock down his pants like he's told, and the Ranger studies the rusted puzzle in his hands that used to be his father's gun.

TWELVE

The Day Roadkill Was Invented

"In Ezekiel's valley of dry bones,
it fell hard and dark to the ground.
It fell without a sound."
-Bruce Springsteen, "Black Cowboys"

Desert. Dusk.

Two black men are riding in silence, a dozen or so townspeople and their dead horses littering the horizon behind them. The men share the idea that no one is following them anymore, that they are the last of the exodus, and they engage in elaborate maintenance on their bridles and horns, crack the joints in their knuckles and necks as nonchalant as possible, treating it as a duty not to display death on their faces. But their haunted eyes betray them both when they come upon a dead dog on the path, and they both know that this first evidence of wagon path is too little too late. The lead rider puts weight in his stirrup to slow his horse and take a longer look.

"First time I ever saw that," he says. "Animals are gonna have to learn to stay off those tracks 'cause there's gonna be more and more things with wheels every day. Getting faster and faster and faster."

"Like your mouth."

"You watch. You'll see."

"Maybe."

"This is something that will be hard to stop. A dog always wants to take the same path as a man. One day, you'll see something like this every hundred feet."

The other cowboy considers this as he snaps his rope to pick up the pace again.

***

Church tent. Same day.

The Preacher stands on a box, expounding to a mob of faces so dust-covered and motionless they're almost invisible against the soiled cloth walls behind them. The Preacher struggles around a cough, further wrecking his throat with wretched dry shouts.

"What more of a sign do people need!" he cries. "We've had a dead horse roaming this goddamn town since the last leaves fell! A dead horse walks past you on the street, and any child can throw a rock clean through the hole in its head, and you don't think that's peculiar? You don't think that's a sign? What more do you want? A black moon? A green sun? A rain of lizards and envy, blood and bile?"

The Preacher steps off his box and walks up to the front row of faces. As he looks real close at their eyes and necks for flutters of life, it's clear about half of them have long since died right where they were sitting, possibly while he was talking. He draws no attention to this, even lays a hand on a woman's dead shoulder as if she's just whispered something inspiring to him, then he goes back to his box. His voice is stronger now.

"But I've been thinking, my brothers and sisters. Thinking hard. This Alcohol Amendment I prospected earlier might not have been the answer. In fact, it might not have made much sense at all. And without water or whiskey to drink, there's only one answer left really, only one thing left in our town to quench our thirst."

The Preacher pauses as he notices Robby peeking his head in again from around a tent flap. Eyes on the boy, he continues his sermon.

"What can quench this thirst? I ask you. Only one thing."

He searches the next couple rows for any sign of life and finds little. Until his next word puts some light back in their eyes.

"Blood."

At the sound of this, eyelids flicker, and some open their

mouths, too, sandpaper tongues across split lips. The savage thirst visible in every face, breaking through every dazed, cloudy gaze. The Preacher points at the boy, his voice now booming.

"You! What brings you here? Speak!"

"Uh, sir, uh, I just had a question."

The Preacher clicks his teeth, then waves the boy on.

"Well, let's hear it."

"Were there guns in the Bible?"

The Preacher's teeth stop clicking around his smile, and he opens his hands to the congregation.

"See that? I forgot my white collar this morning, but this young man recognizes a man of God without the uniform! Or does he? With a crazy question like that I'm not so sure. So, to answer you... of course there were guns in the Bible. Only they didn't use 'gun.' They used other words, like 'rock,' or 'jealousy,' or 'love.' Tear out every page with *those* words and circle them and you've found all the guns they were hiding in there. For example..."

He stops to hack another cough and launches a gray, mouse-sized ball of snot into the air, and now his voice is rattling again.

"'*Love, for thy day is near. Let no debt remain outstanding, except the continuing debt to love one another, for he who loves his fellow man has fulfilled the law. Love your neighbor as yourself. Love does no harm to its neighbor. Therefore love is the fulfillment of the law...*'"

Pause, but the cough never comes. "Wait. Wait! What half of the book is this? This is New Testament shit! Did you not see me tear the Book right the hell down the middle?"

Eyes closed, he rubs his knobby head in frustration.

"Anyhow, now, you can take that quote and scratch the word 'gun' over all those 'loves.' See that? It works. And that's a lot of goddamn guns."

"So it's supposed to be '*Gun* thy neighbor?'" Robby mumbles, unconvinced. The Preacher's eyes go wide.

"Damn right. You know, boy, that line in 'Romans' always confused me before today, but I think you're onto something here. 'Gun' can be used just like 'love.' It's a verb and a noun, too. And

I thought I had nothing left to learn in the Book! Thank ya, boy!" Then his eyes narrow, threatening. "Now get the everlovin' fuck out of here. We're talking about God like he's not here. And that's the rudest thing any man can do to his Father."

"Why?"

"Why? Maybe you ought to worry about how what you're doing right now ain't right in the Lord's house neither. Tell me, son, why do you have your limsy hands down your pants?"

Suddenly inspired, the Preacher steps forward again and takes a gun from a corpse on a crate in the front row. Then, with a dramatic flourish, he grabs a handful of the tent cloth, kicks at a post, and brings the walls billowing down around him like an enormous cape. Sunlight explodes across all the faces, alive and dead, and a cloud of yellow dust swells around their circle. Three men and two women, bodies soaked in gallons of whiskey, ignite in this blaze of light and begin to burn, silently screaming, no spit in their throats to loosen their vocal cords. Leathery skeletons of bone and ash are all that remain. The horrific emulations barely register in the alcohol drenched brains of the dying congregation.

The Preacher points his gun at the sky until his eyes adjust to the glare and he can see the sun burning on the tip of his barrel. He cocks the hammer.

"Where is He? I'm gonna 'love' him for y'all. Wait, I think I see... there you are..."

He fires his gun at the sun. The shot is so loud, the Preacher's ears rattle, and he turns to count faces to make sure no more of his flock burst into kindling.

"Don't be shocked by the thunder. Yes, I've fired a bullet at God, but that only shows that I have more faith today than I did yesterday. Why? Because I wouldn't try to kill someone that I didn't think existed. Friends, this is *truly* the happiest day of my life!"

As his ears stop ringing, the Preacher notices Robby again, and the boy releases his gun-shaped rock in his pants pocket then starts running. The Preacher calls after him.

"Laddy, don't you ever come back around here again, lest you got something to drink! And we know you do. You're looking more and more like a drumstick with every day that passes."

A dead mouth in the back starts singing stronger than the Preacher thought possible.

"*A man on a pale horse. And the man that sat upon him was death. And hell followed with him...*"

***

Porch. Sunset.

McKenna and the Ranger tap their toes and heels in unison as they creak on a lacquered Cherrywood swing, the sun a bloodshot eye on the horizon.

"Why'd you send me that letter?" he asks her.

McKenna looks surprised for a second then shakes her head and takes his hand.

"I didn't send you a letter. Robby musta done that."

"Your boy knows who I am?"

"He picked up on some things, heard me talking. Talking about being run out of town."

"You left Bisbée, 'Kenna."

"I left because I didn't want a brother to kill a lover. Or a father to kill a brother. Or vice versa. Who can keep track?"

The Ranger studies his hand.

"Is that why you're here? Or is it that other reason."

"Why do you keep asking me that?" he says, taking his hand back.

"Listen to me, Bob. I'm the one you're looking for."

He crosses his arms, interested in what she's saying.

"By that, I mean I'm responsible for Gray's death, not Red. And Gray knew about Red. And he had a plan to keep me all to himself."

She fades off, unable to continue, rubbing the memory of life in her belly. The Ranger stares a moment, then takes his hat off for the first time. His steel gray hair crawls over his ruddy ears, a white line on his forehead divides his sunburned face from his skull.

"Is he still here?"

She doesn't ask who he means, Red or Gray. She only closes her eyes, and suddenly the Ranger knows he's about to hear it all.

"Tell me everything," he says.

THIRTEEN

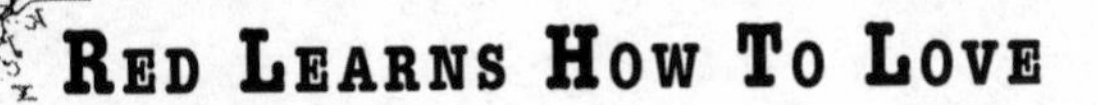

Red Learns How To Love

"They say I shot a man named Gray and took his wife to Italy.
She inherited a million bucks, and when she died it came to me.
I can't help it if I'm lucky."
-Bob Dylan, "Idiot Wind"

Agua Fría. Weeks ago, but seems like years.

Gray Wendler is standing in the middle of a circle of bickering townspeople. Gray scratches his face wearily then puts two fingers in his mouth and whistles. A horse cuts its way through the crowd, recognizable to everyone as Red's white Palomino. The horse is bright-white, clear-eyed, and strong, snorting and stamping a hoof and shaking a fly off its ear. It gives no indication that it's about to be shot through the head. Gray mounts it and turns it around. McKenna and Robby are standing toward the back of the crowd.

"If you start leaving town this month," he says to them all. "You'll have enough water to carry on the journey. But if you put it off too long, the trip will get drier and drier. Just like this town, everyone dropped and dusted."

Indistinct arguing begins to rise from the crowd and gain momentum. McKenna pulls Robby in closer to her legs. Gray turns his horse to look at everyone, and his voice gets louder.

"You have to listen to me! We've had three more wells dry up this week. This town is dying. You have to think about where y'all are gonna go."

"Bullshit," scoffs a muffled voice in the back.

Gray turns his horse again and sees Red pushing through the crowd. Red stops in front of a man with a dirty blue cap with an American flag stitched into it, shredded leather saddlebags over each shoulder. Red grabs the man's coat collar and stuffs a long package into one of his bags. Smiling, Red lightly slaps the man's face.

"Make sure that gets delivered on your way out," he says. "Thanks, boy."

Red pushes past the mailman and steps forward into the circle. Gray's horse is startled by Red and flares its nostrils at him in anger, and Red stumbles back a step, then comes forward again. Red puts two fingers in his mouth and tries to imitate Gray's whistling. Instead he spits all over and the horse whirls around and rears up, even more spooked, and Gray works to steady it.

"What was that you said?"

"You heard me, you lyin' mutton-puncher," Red spits. "And I'll say it again. Bullshit."

They stare at each other a minute, then Red laughs.

"You know what? I've seen a dog come when you whistle, even your wife. Never a horse though. How'd you do that?"

Anticipating trouble, the crowd behind Gray begins to thin, as does the crowd around Red, who turns to face the scattering townspeople.

"I think our sheriff here don't really give a shit about water, or you and I. I think our man here is hiding something."

The crowd murmurs and look to each other, then up at Gray. Robby shrinks behind his mother's knee.

"I don't know what this man's talking about," Gray says. "But you're gambling with your lives if you stay here. This town is—"

"Naw, I think I'll gamble with *my* life, thanks!" Red yells. "And I'll gamble that you ain't going anywhere at all."

"What are you saying?" Gray's horse spins, sensing his anger, and he struggles to keep it steady.

"I saw you," Red says, pointing. "Last night. And three nights before that. You were creaking around behind houses with a wheelbarrow. I got you nailed. To the counter, sir, as they say."

The townspeople grumble louder, and now all eyes are on Gray.

"You were digging somewhere," Red continues. "Or digging

everywhere. Either way, you were looking for something."

Gray shakes his head, laughs.

"You're wrong. You're so wrong you don't know how wrong you are. You're so wrong you're dangerous."

"That may be true. It just seems to me that you want to send all these good people into the desert with your word instead of water. Tell me something. What's buried here that's got our true blue sheriff risking all our lives?"

The talk of "true blue" sends an angry ripple through the crowd, an obvious reference to Gray's rumored past of fighting for the North during the War. Some still didn't appreciate the color he'd recently adopted for a nickname. He scowls, hand not on his gun yet, but fingers fluttering like they're thinking about it.

"Red, don't act like you give a shit about these people today. It just doesn't suit you."

Everyone is shouting over each other now, making it hard for the two men to keep arguing. Questions start flying from the crowd, worried folk demanding answers.

"What's he mean, Sheriff?"

"What're you hidin'?"

Gray holds up a hand to soothe them.

"Listen, listen. Listen to me. There's no getting around the facts here." He points to a man in back. "John, your well dried up last Sunday, am I right? I checked three nights in a row after that, and didn't get even a drop in the bucket. We know this is happening."

Another growing grumble of murmurs, and the crowd starts to move in on Gray and his horse. Red takes the opportunity to split the distance between him and McKenna and her son.

"Gray, your wife sure don't look like she's taking her nipper anywhere," Red laughs. "And, you know, sticking around town like that? Dang, that seems kinda dangerous, with a child 'n' all. That's sure no way to take care of my son. Oh, I'm sorry, *our* son."

Gray's eyes narrow, and his hand moves towards his weapon. The crowd quiets fast when they see Red's gun has already cleared its holster. Gray looks around, unsure what to do, then moves his hand away from his holster. Red barks a laugh, then drops his arm to aim at Gray's horse's head instead. Robby runs from behind McKenna, eyes wide, hands out.

"No!"

Red ignores the boy, staring into the horse's clear, brown eyes. Lighting flashes in the distance, always the tease. This time there's no thunder.

"Don't do it," Gray says, and Red seems to consider this, realizing the crossroads they're on. Then the thunder rumbles and he's smiling big again.

"You hear that? It's gonna rain. There'll be plenty to drink besides nose paint. Especially if you're face-up on the ground, mouth open and waiting for it."

The crowd backs off even further, and Red puts his gun to the side of the horse's head. He closes one eye, and the horse does, too, seemingly aware of its fate.

"Red…"

"What do you care? If you ain't going anywhere, why do you need a horse?"

"…don't..."

Red fires. The front right leg of the horse buckles, the impact rolling through its muscles like a wave. It lurches forward a step, slumps, and stays this way a moment.

Then the horse stands back up straight. It turns and blinks at Red, and now Red is the one who takes a step back. He stares, gun smoking, as blood runs from a hole in the horse's head, right behind its eye. It turns its head towards him slowly, so both eyes are on him. The crowd is dead silent, a couple people even run, and Red's gun hand starts to shake and he angrily shoves his pistol back in the holster. He stares, shaking his head and waiting for the horse to drop.

"First horse I ever killed," he mutters. "And it won't fall."

"God will damn you," Gray says, gun out, tracing a line toward Red. But Red is still as fast as he ever was, and his gun is back up and in Gray's face before his finger can squeeze.

"Let's see if you know that trick, too," Red says, the last thing Gray will ever hear, as a bullet blows through Gray's wide eye like a locomotive. McKenna screams as Gray's hat rides a cloud of blood and brains to the ground behind him, and he tumbles back out of his saddle, joints now loose like a puppet with its strings clipped. Everyone is pretty much running now, and the Preacher drags a screaming McKenna off the street, while she pulls Robby with her, hate burning through his tears.

Red steps over to Gray's body and gives it an investigative kick, then turns back to the horse, clearly haunted by its refusal to behave like something that's been shot through the head. After biting his lip a moment, he puts away his gun and slowly swings himself up onto the animal's back, into Gray's old saddle. He strokes its mane, his hand streaking the long blonde hairs with stripes of red. He digs a heel into its haunches and it starts to trot, slow, like it's underwater, rolling its neck and snorting great red ropes of blood from its skull and nostrils. With every step, they both seem to grow stronger.

Red and his dead horse ride away into the night.

FOURTEEN

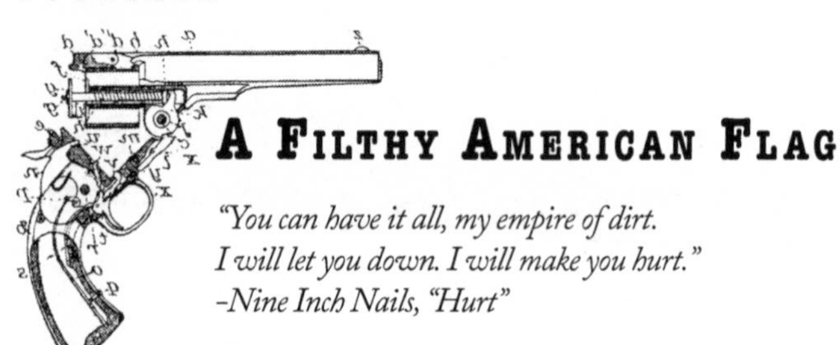

A Filthy American Flag

"You can have it all, my empire of dirt.
I will let you down. I will make you hurt."
-Nine Inch Nails, "Hurt"

Agua Fría. Happening right now.

The Ranger and Tom are stockpiling supplies on McKenna's porch. Sweating, the Ranger drops his coat on some saddlebags and goes back into the house. Tom takes the opportunity to dig through his pockets and comes up with the poster he'd tucked away back in Bisbée. Tom unfolds, then unrolls it, then holds it out in front of him with both hands. He squints as he reads, shaking his head in amazement, then laughing outright. The Ranger walks up behind him to look over his shoulder, and Tom begins to read out loud, adding his own embellishments.

"'Wanted! For the murder of one white Palomino stallion, three lizards, various flies... oh yeah, and Gray Wendler. Reward... five bucks. Or three pesos.'"

Tom crumples the poster in his fist and cocks his head to the Ranger behind him.

"That's kind of insulting to Gray and his family, ain't it? I mean, think of the flies."

"Palomino is a color, not a breed," the Ranger says.

"Not to mention the fact that Red's sketch seems to be..." Tom squints again. "I don't know. What exactly is he doing in that picture?"

"Kicking a chicken."

"Right. No babies nearby?"

"Red made that poster as a joke," the Ranger says, turning away.

"Sent it to me. Back before he killed anybody, I reckon."

"More like you wreckin'," Tom coughs, rolling the poster back up, then folding it in half. Then in half again. He struggles to fold it a third time.

"I didn't know Palominos could be white," he says to himself. Then to the Ranger, "Hey, did you know that you can't fold anything in half more than five times?"

"Don't you mean 'tear' anything in half?"

"I don't remember. Sounds right though. You ever try to tear anything in half more than once?"

"Just the Bible."

"Me, too!" Tom laughs. "Oh, hey, tell me again why you stopped at a gun store on the way here and didn't bring a gun that works."

The Ranger walks to the end of the porch, staring at the sky.

"Tom, did I ever tell you why my dad was fired from Smith & Wesson Incorporated?"

"Nope, not that I recall."

"Well, he was stealing random parts from guns so that he could take all those springs and pins and screws and put together his own pistol one day. Only the parts were from twelve different guns, and these puzzle pieces didn't fit together at all when he finally sat down to do it. So he got frustrated and stole all twelve of those guns instead. That was his last day working for anyone. And that same day he started his special calendar."

"I heard about that calendar. Whole family's a bag of nails. This is why you never know what day it is. This is why we're not already on the road out of here."

"You don't need to know the day, Tom. All you need is the year for making any big decision. Maybe the hour. Sometimes the hour."

Tom shrugs and opens his own gun to check the cylinder.

"Well, I got the only timepiece we need right here. And five bucks is five bucks! It'll pay for his bullet, anyway." Tom snaps the cylinder shut, satisfied. "Where do you think Red's hiding? You know what, don't answer that. I'll find that nibbler before you finish packin' your reloading outfit. And I'll just go ahead and wrap this shit up before I get sick of thinking about it or listening to you reminisce."

Tom holsters his gun and pulls his hat down tight. He leans in to catch the Ranger's eyes.

"You ever think about all these names in this town?" he asks. "Red? Gray? All we need is a 'Blue' and we got ourselves an American flag."

"It'd sure be a filthy one."

***

At the ass end of town, Red's crew mills around like headless chickens, circling a gnarly dead tree, cackling and high-stepping around the corpses of townspeople piled in the shade. They're drunk, dying, but positively giddy. Jackass is cutting off sections from a tangle of frayed rope at his feet, adding them to his collection of nooses. One lonely noose still hangs from the lowest branch of the tree, and Little Joe climbs onto the dead pile to put his head inside and pull it tight. Egg sits silent with his back to the trunk, watching it all, while Red leans against the other side. Mud sees Little Joe in the noose and lunges forward, shoving Little Joe off the bodies, and everyone laughs when the dry rope snaps.

"Hey!" shouts Little Joe.

"Don't worry, kid," Red says without looking up. "That rope's about as dry as my tongue right now. You ain't in no real danger." He kicks at a dead farmer near his boot. "Hey, grab that one. I always hated that bastard. String his ass up! Which one of you owl hoots can tie the best California collar?"

Mud and Jackass pull the man off the pile and struggle to get his head into another noose. They throw the rope over the branch, and once the rope is tight, they both jump back to let the body swing. But this time the rope doesn't snap, and it creaks and stretches the corpse's neck until the head pops off and flies up into the tree, ricocheting around the dead branches until it finally smacks the ground and rolls away to soak up the sunshine.

"Jesus Christ!" Mud yells, jumping back from the head. "Would that even happen?"

"Just did, didn't it?" Little Joe says, getting away from the body, too. "Dang! Told you that shit was dangerous! You nigh unto killed me."

"Then why the fuck did you put your head in that hemp?" Red asks, still not looking up.

"I don't know. The same reason we're hanging corpses?"

"Good answer."

The men share a laugh, and uncork another bottle, as Jackass drags the headless body out of the shade. The dead man's pants rip loose in his hands, and Jackass hacks and drops everything in horror when he sees the legs are still inside them.

"What the hell?" Jackass says, hand over his mouth. "Maybe a better question would be… why the hell would some cottonwood blossom continue to shit sand?"

"Hey!" Red says, finally looking up from under his hat. "Any of you hangdogs wanna go kill that crazy fucking Preacher before we die?"

No one says anything, and Red shrugs and sighs and hides back under his hat, and Little Joe takes a swing at Mud when he walks by him. Mud dodges it easily, then grabs his arm and shoves him backwards into the bodies. Little Joe gives him a murderous stare as he works to unwrap himself from the black skin and stink, fumbling for his belt and his weapon.

"You sure you wanna try that?" Mud says. "'Cause if you miss, you better sleep standing up for the rest of your life because one day you'll wake up and I'll be standing there too and on that day..."

Red kicks some dirt at Mud.

"Shut that shit up," he says, "Tired of fucking about this trio." He walks over to help up Little Joe.

"You know who you remind me of?" Red asks. "Egg was once the kinda kid that followed me around. It was back in Bisbée, weren't it? And he was even smaller than you back then, if you can believe it. More like a fragile robin's egg than the sturdy chicken bullet is he now. See, everyone gets one of those, a second shadow like Egg. And the shadow that follows you around, well, sometimes it becomes too important for its vocation. See, a 'protégé' is really another word for a problem. And three shadows? Well, that's three problems, and that shit's downright dangerous."

"What the hell are you talking about?" Egg says from his side of the tree. "I wasn't no shadow."

"Yeah, you were, Biscuit Man. You were my second shadow all right. Still are. Luckily, it was easy to tell these shadows apart. Yours was the one with all the spiders in it."

"What did you call me? I never been caught squeezing no biscuit nor choking no saddle horn in my life."

"What did you say?"

"Huh?"

"Is there a difference between the two?"

"What?"

"Wait, how were you using that word?"

"I..."

"Shut up."

Egg says nothing, instead starts gouging the bark with his knife again.

"Anyone know who lives in the last house on the left side of Main Street?" Jackass says after a long drink.

"No one," Red says.

"How do you know?"

"Because that was the sixth man I killed. Burned down his house, too, if I recall correct."

"Did he have a boy?"

"Nope. Just a dog. I didn't kill the dog."

Jackass frowns in confusion and takes a longer drink.

"Okay!" Red says, pushing off the tree. "Anyone know where there's any horses around here to drink?"

"I am fascinated that I now exist in a world where people talk of 'drinking horses' like it's nothing," Jackass muses.

"How can you be sure?" someone asks.

"Last horse around is that dead one you've been riding," Egg says, and Jackass scratches his head, trying to focus.

"I thought we were looking for something," he mumbles.

"You *sure* there ain't no horses 'round here?" Red says. "Thought I heard some horses this morning."

"Why all the fuckin' talk about horses? I hate them things."

"Horses are the key! Towns run on horses! Listen, you goddamn crackers. We're running out of time. I think. And I get the feeling some nobby strangers rode in here recently, don't you? And that's more horses. We might need to drink them horses to make it to the end."

"You mean get them horses to drink?"

"What did he say?"

"Make it to the end of what?"

"No, I said 'drink the horses.'"

"Drink the horses, okay," Egg says. "What about your horse? Drink that one you're so thirsty."

"There ain't nothing to drink in that horse. That beautiful horse of mine runs on pure hate. And hate is dry as a bone. That reminds me. Anybody seen my baby? Someone go find my ride! Keeps wandering off. I don't think it can see much, even with that third eye, despite what them Hindus say."

"Make it to the end of what?" Jackass says again.

"What do you think?"

"Red, I think drinking whiskey instead of water hurts my head. And I'm hurting so bad I've been thinking about popping it off on one of these ropes. Rolling it out there to bake next to that one. Or that one. Do I need my head for what you got planned, boss?"

"Yes," he says. "Please hold onto to your head for now."

"How much time you think we got left?" Little Joe asks, serious. Red answers, serious for once, too.

"Enough."

FIFTEEN

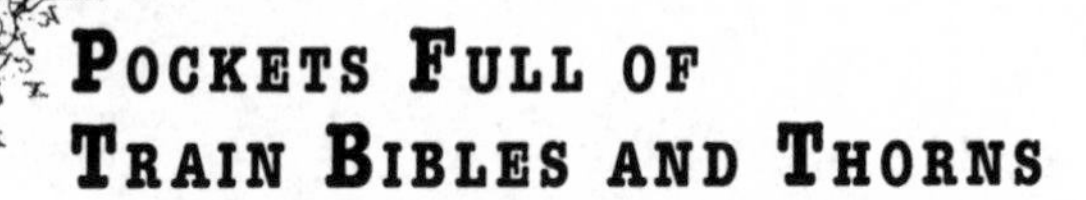

Pockets Full of Train Bibles and Thorns

"Remember the morning we dug up your gun,
the worms in the barrel, the setting sun."
-Bruce Springsteen, "Devil's Arcade"

Tom is alone, riding slowly through the hazy nucleus of the town. Weaving his horse through the deserted main road, he heads up to the smoking storefronts to systematically look inside every one. As he approaches the last couple burning buildings, his horse bucks, spooked, and Little Joe crashes out the door with a stack of candy bars crushed in a fist and a huge rainbow sucker jutting from his mouth. Little Joe freezes and stares up at Tom's gun, out and ready. The sucker drops from his mouth and thumps the ground in a puff of dust. Tom's gun dips.

"Go ahead and pick up your candy, son. You can still eat it. Just wipe off the dirt."

Little Joe picks up the sucker and holds it like a weapon.

"Ain't no dirt on that, dummy!" he says. "Ain't got enough spit around here to stick to anything."

Tom sees the sucker is indeed dry as a bone, and he starts to reach back for his canteen when Robby suddenly turns a corner and startles them both. When Tom turns back around, Little Joe's gun is out and pointing at his face.

"What the hell are you doing, boy?" Tom says to Robby, still staring at Little Joe, bringing his own gun back up. "You and your ma are supposed to be packin' up." Then, to Little Joe, "Easy, kid. Don't make me shoot you. I don't want your candy, so you can relax."

They stare at each other, dead silent, and Little Joe's gun starts to shake. Tom notices Little Joe's hesitation and starts to lower his weapon.

"Listen up. I'm not gonna shoot anybody here. I'm just looking for Red. Or the groggery. You want to learn how to drink, kid?"

Little Joe lets his gun hang down by his side, then whips his head toward Robby fast as a snake.

"Red's busy. In fact, he's been busy trying to find what this little bastard here's been hiding."

"We ain't hiding nothing!"

"How old are you, kid?" Tom wants to know. "Even the children go heeled around here, huh? Are the cats packin', too?"

Little Joe ignores him, still throwing accusations at Robby.

"Yeah, right, hiding nothing. That's why you and your ma are wrangling all those horses in the barn. That's why you and your ma are the only two people in town who can still run and break a sweat while doing it! That Calico bitch is hiding plenty."

Robby balls his fists and starts toward Little Joe. Little Joe just laughs and throws his gun away into the street. Then he drops the rest of his candy bars and balls his fists, too. Tom holsters his pistol and leans back in his saddle.

"Fine, you wanna fight?" Little Joe shrugs. "We'll fight." He yells up at Tom. "Don't stop us neither! We're the same age."

Tom laughs in disbelief at this. But as he narrows his eyes to look closer, he's horrified by Little Joe's unhealthy appearance and the possible truth of such a statement.

"How old are you really, kid?" he asks again. Little Joe just grins, teeth taking up half his face like a coyote's skull.

"Thought I was older, huh? Yeah, everyone thinks water is so good for you, helps you grow strong? Fuck no! Take away water and you jump ahead about ten years. If I'd have known that, I'd have stopped drinking it sooner, and I'd be your age by now, mister. Hey, Robby, I missed you at school today. Hold this."

Little Joe throws a wild punch and catches Robby on the top of the head. Robby falls down, and Little Joe is on his back quick, rabbit-punching him in the spine. Robby struggles to get up, then starts scratching at the dirt under him. Tom dismounts and runs over, grabbing Little Joe by the back of his belt and the collar of his coat. He throws Little Joe ten feet down the street, shaking his head at how far the kid flew.

"You're dead, you fuckin' acorn."

"No, you're fucking dead, kid," Tom says, spitting on the ground. "You sure ain't alive. Throwing you was like throwing a dead rat. Shit, more like throwing half a rat! Look at you. An out-and-out scarecrow, walking around, startin' shit."

Little Joe brushes himself off as he runs to grab his pistol from the street. Tom watches him close as he picks it up and reholsters, eyes blazing, then turns and sprints away. Tom leans down and hauls Robby up off the ground, straightening the boy's twisted shirt and folding his collar back down.

"If you're gonna grab a handful of dirt, you should throw it in his eyes, buddy," Tom says. "But be straight, was that kid right about them horses? You and your mama got some steeds in that barn?"

Robby doesn't answer, and Tom, still feeling paternal, pulls one of the boy's naked arms back through a flapping flannel sleeve where it had slipped out.

"Either your shirt is growing, or you're shrinking, little man."

"It was my dad's shirt."

"I see. So, did I hear a train whistle last night? Are there tracks around here?"

"No, sir. There ain't never been a train through here. You must have heard some animal whistling or something. Mind playing tricks on ya. Like with them horses people keep hearin'."

"Uh huh."

Tom steps back, brushing a final clump of dirt from the boy's hair. Robby looks up at Tom affectionately, then goes back to the spot where he was being pummeled and starts digging again.

"What are you burying, squirrel?"

"Burying nothing, I was trying to pull this loose."

Robby wrestles a small rock from the dirt and holds it out to

Tom, who takes it to study. It's vaguely heart-shaped, a penny dreadful heart from his childhood funny books, not the hearts Tom had seen buzzards wrestle from dehydrated livestock. Real hearts were shaped like nothing. Tom flips it over a couple times, then tucks it into Robby's front shirt pocket and affectionately rubs his head. Robby steps back as Tom checks his gun and climbs back on his horse.

"You on the prod?"

"Maybe."

"You're going after Red, ain't you?"

"Just go home, Robby."

"I've been all over the town these last two days. I'll bet I can find him first."

"Damn it, boy. You get home now," Tom tries on a serious look. "You take your heart, and you put it somewhere safe."

Robby backs up, a look on his face like he's ready to run again.

"Don't worry. I'll find him first, and I'll save your life. I owe you, sir."

"Hold on now."

Robby stares at Tom, looking like he's almost but not quite ready to spill all sorts of confidential, clandestine reports. Then he unloads them all.

"Okay, I'll tell you a secret, but keep it dry and don't tell my mother. I had this idea yesterday, see. I've been filling Red's holster with thorns. While he's sleeping. I know where they hold up, and him and his gang are so far gone with their whiskey, I could probably do it while he was awake. Even though he's been cooking in the sun, he's still faster than anyone. But the thorns will slow him down a bit. Enough for you to get off a shot anyway."

"Oh, my God," Tom blinks slow. "Listen to me close now. Do not go near them again. We are leaving today. Time to pull foot. I should have known I wasn't gonna be pulling in the pieces on this job. Now run, boy! Go!"

Robby runs.

"I can do it!" he shouts while high-stepping backwards. "He's been painting his tonsils for thirteen days and counting! And I've been soaking his coat in whiskey since Sunday, so don't smoke around him neither."

Tom spins and heels his mount to give chase, but the boy vanishes behind the smoldering stores.

"What the hell is wrong with the kids around here?" he asks a town held together by smoke.

***

The Ranger and McKenna stand on her porch steps, a worried look on his face, a horrified look on hers. Something the Ranger's just said still hovers in the air between them.

"How long?" she asks him.

"I don't know. Don't matter. Long enough to do what I need to do."

"I can't think about that right now," McKenna says, shaking her head. "We have to find Robby. This time, he ain't leaving my sight. Once I get a hold of that boy, I'm tying him to a wagon wheel, and he's going to cartwheel right alongside me when we roll out past the city limits."

The Ranger adjusts the guns on his belt so they're level, then shields his eyes to check the sun and his internal clock. He's thinking about young men and how towns get strange with them running amok with no rules. Then he thinks about how towns would be even stranger without them.

"Save the other wheel for Tom."

***

Tying his horse to the hitching post, Tom claps its neck goodbye and turns to the smoldering farmhouse, hand over his gun. Excited by the sounds of muffled laughter and shattering glass, his heart skips a beat when a mud-covered man with skin split and pitted as jerk steak bumbles into sight from around back. The man stops and shakes his head hard to try sobering up. Tom's gun comes out, slowly tracing his outline. Hands high, no attempt to clear leather, the man moves back, almost tripping over a tipped wheelbarrow of sand, stopping with his tailbone against a sagging stone well. Eyes still locked on the weapon, the man tries to spit but nothing comes out except a sputtering rant that Tom has heard too many times before.

"Don't know who you are, or how you got the drop on me, but you just better watch your back, boy. You just better sleep with one eye open. 'Cause one day, when you least expect it, when you're relaxed and sitting on the shitter or playing cards or telling your frogs a bedtime story, or maybe all three at the same time, I'm gonna be there, right behind you, and on that day I'm gonna—"

Tom fires, his nostrils eagerly sucking gunpowder as a spinning Catherine Wheel of blood and meat explodes from every worn seam and crack in the man's hat.

"No, you're not."

Mud's nearly headless corpse collapses backwards into the well, his last sliver of throat lolling with the reckless weight of a newborn's skull, just as another man, all smiling eyes, teeth and orange hair, crashes out the front door.

"Hello, Red," Tom says. "You finally thirsty enough to rail it?"

"No trains come through here," Red says, glancing toward the well.

"There's other ways outta town, I reckon."

"Where's Mud?" Red asks.

There's a splash as the body finally hits bottom. At the unexpected sound of water, Tom's eyes flare and Red's smile slips, his right hand flexing over his holster, cracking the knuckles of his trigger finger with his thumb, click, click, waiting, waiting.

But Tom can't help turning toward the first sign of water in days, and Red pulls, burying a bullet deep in his chest.

Tom backs up to sit on the edge of the well, body curling like a bug. Red strides over, then stops to notice his shooting hand is bleeding.

"The hell?" he mutters, fingers wiggling. "How'd you do that?"

Red blinks in amazement at the bloody thorns magically riddling his skin, then upends Tom to join the man he killed.

Suddenly, a skeletal, emaciated boy is standing there. And when the second splash comes, the boy's eyes positively bulge at the sound, lips rolling back over long sharp teeth, and he reaches for the bucket. Red can't believe a child has survived in his town so long. He fires another bullet so things start making sense again. The boy slumps, and Red catches him with a forearm, dumping him down the well next. Another splash.

"Ain't you supposed to be in school?" he yells after the boy, followed by, "Mud, do you see him, too?"

Then he whistles hard over bloody fingers, and Tom's horse turns the corner, ears cocked, dragging a dead limb from its post. Without hesitation, Red walks up and puts his gun behind the horse's eye.

Boom.

The horse thumps forward on its knees, then collapses into a thick mushroom of dust.

Another man walks out of the house, his mouth cracked and pulsing like a fish on the floor.

"Who shot who?" Egg asks, then runs for the well. "More important, did I just hear water?"

Red smiles and steps in front of Egg, grabs the bucket off the crank, and drops it into the dark. The handle spins as the rope unrolls, and Egg licks his split lips in anticipation.

The bucket hits the bodies at the bottom with a distant thud.

Crushed, Egg sits down hard, kicking dirt like a kid.

"Sorry, sir," Red says. "You heard it. Dry as bone, just like the rest. Now go find Mud. Don't know where that cocksucker went."

Egg pulls out a bottle of whiskey, dropping it when he hears the hissing of dead air from the nostrils of the freshly killed horse. He kneels next to it and puts a finger into the new hole in its skull. He licks off the blood with a satisfied sigh.

"Hey, did you see that dog that came back here?" he asks after another finger.

"Huh? No, just your horse there. Ain't no dogs left around here. Kids neither."

"Hey, you seen Mud?"

"Huh? No. You crazy? You can't have mud without any water!"

"The hell does that mean?"

"I don't know. Go find his ass," Red sneers. "You're asking a lot of questions for someone dying of thirst."

Egg stops fingering the horse's head and stands back up.

"You know, Red, usually when you hear that kinda thud at the bottom of a well, it's because you're dropping honey buckets by mistake."

"Dropping what?" Red asks without interest.

"Honey buckets. It's what they call a bucket that moves shit in the wrong direction. Sorta' like an outhouse. 'Cept you dump in the bucket and drop it down. And when the well fills up and there's no more splash, your rum-hole's done."

Red's laughing, like always.

"Then that's exactly what this is!"

***

Robby walks through dead, sagging corn stalks, holding the extra length of sleeves on his father's shirt up to his nose to stop the bleeding. He slows down as the small shadow of a boy approaches on the horizon. The boy is walking in front of the setting sun, and even with his hand shielding his eyes, Robby initially believes he's casting a shadow much longer than normal. Then they intersect, and his shadow holds out a hand with a shredded half Bible fluttering in the hot wind between them. Robby reaches out to take it, but his shadow won't let it go. It points to Robby's front shirt pocket instead, and Robby pulls out the heart-shaped rock and hands it over. Only then does the shadow release the pages, and Robby takes them eagerly, pushing them into the pocket left vacant by his heart stone. The large Bible pages slip into his father's giant shirt, next to Robby's thorns with room to spare. Robby remembers when Gray gave him the shirt, stopping to pull three decks of cards from that pocket. Him and the poker players down at the groggery called them "train bibles," a term that rattled around Robby's head like a corn kernel every time he heard it.

When Robby looks up, his shadow is back under his feet where it goes and instead he glimpses a dog disappearing back over the hill. He pats his father's pocket to make sure the pages are really there, then sees two figures approaching from the west, their long shadows stretching out to meet him a good five minutes before they do. Bobby's still studying the ground when McKenna grabs him by the chin to meet her stare.

"Where were you?" she asks, frantic. "What's this ruckus?"

"It's okay. I'm okay," Robby huffs as the Ranger grabs his shoulders and spins him around.

"Look at me, boy," the Ranger says. "Where's my deputy?"

"He went to find Red."

"Red?" The Ranger's head drops at the name. "Where? Nevermind. We're leaving."

Robby reaches into his huge pocket and shows them a thorn.

"No, no, look. it's okay. He'll be okay. I slowed him down!"

"I said we're leaving," the Ranger says again, releasing Robby. He tugs on the Ranger's hand, still trying to show them the thorn.

"No, look. Tom can beat him now. I foxed him. They sleep a lot, and last time they slept, I filled up his holster with these. He'll get hung up. It'll slow him down, I swear."

The Ranger shakes his head and turns to McKenna.

"We're leaving Agua Fría. Right now. As soon as we get your horses. No more swearin'. Time to paddle."

"But if they already—"

"Listen, I swore I'd get you, and that's what I'm gonna do. Three days without water is the limit."

"I thought you said no more swearing."

The Ranger stares at his hands, feeling them shrink inside his gloves to the size they were when he was a boy. His shooting hand begins to shake in anticipation of future failures.

"What about Tom?" she asks him.

"If he found Red, he'll be staying."

SIXTEEN

The Day Graffiti Was Invented

"You wired me awake and hit me with a hand of broken nails. You tied my lead and pulled my chain to watch my blood begin to boil. But I'm gonna break my rusty cage and run."
-Soundgarden, "Rusty Cage"

Egg, Red, Jackass, and Little Joe are walking through the stretch of woods along the edge of Agua Fría. Red studies Jackass like he's made of meat. Little Joe rubs the scabs on his knuckles thoughtfully, while Egg shuffles with his eyes closed, hands out, fingers brushing the dry, hollow trunks as they pass. Egg's eyes spring open as his fingers recognize the area, and he sucks in his breath excited and starts pounding the wood. Everyone looks over to see "**E.G.G.**" carved deep into every tree, in some spots covering every inch, down to the exposed roots and almost eight feet up, higher than any normal man could reach, higher than any dying man could jump. Egg trots out in front of the other two men, and, as Red and Little Joe watch, he steps up to a monstrous dead spruce and, to their amazement, shoves it over easily. Red is shocked and for an instant looks at Egg with something resembling respect.

"How the fuck did you..." Red starts.

"Wanna see it again?" Egg smiles, stepping up to another tree and shouldering it over with a popping, splintering crash.

"Holy shit buckets," Little Joe whispers.

"I agree with that," Jackass says. "Holy. Shit."

Skeptical, Red steps forward to push on his own tree. It doesn't budge.

"No. Try this one."

Egg claps a nearby white trunk with the palm of his hand, and Red walks over, mouth pinched shut, almost petulant. Around the tree is Egg's name again and again, gouged fingernail deep and wrapping the trunk like ribbon. Red leans into it with his shoulder, and wood snaps like firecrackers as it rocks back and forth then steadies.

"How long you been putting your name on these, Egg?" asks Jackass.

"Uh, about six... six..." he stutters. "Sixteen... years."

"And why is that?" asks Little Joe.

"Dunno'," he shrugs, tongue darting. "It was a dumb idea I had once."

"Once?" Mud laughs. "For sixteen years? Sounds more like a dumb idea you keep having!"

"What idea?" asks Red, listening close, then he jerks his head back like he smelled something bad, looking Mud up and down. Everybody else does, too. "When did you get back, Mud?"

"Back from what?"

"Didn't you..." Red trails off, pondering something mostly to himself. "...fuck it. Maybe he swallowed a coin at the bottom of that well. You swallow one of my coins at the bottom of that well, Mud?"

"Huh? Bottom of what?"

"Always knew you were a bad penny, Mud." Egg says. "Turnin' back up like this."

"That's me! Henny Penny!" Mud laughs, putting both hands over his flattened hat. "Wait, who's a penny?"

"You know, come to think of it," Red goes on. "Gray's horse drunk from that well, too. No, no, no, shit better not be making that kinda sense." Then he says to Mud, "Don't worry, son, I'm truly glad to see you again, but it'll hurt twice as bad the second time you go down."

"What y'all talkin' about?" Mud says, scratching a curiously dry hole in his neck.

"Nothin'." Egg says, shrugging and shaking off the conversation, trying not to look at his neck and the lack of blood or mud. Instead, he points back to the house they just left behind.

"You remember way back before everything, back before you killed Gray, when it was common knowledge Gray Wendler had the best five horses in the state? But no one could ever steal those horses of his 'cause, even though he only got around to building half a fence, he didn't need any security at all around the back and the sides. Well, it's this line of trees right here, the only trees in town. That's his security. He thought God built his very own fence for him, and maybe that was true back before everything, back when these trees were alive like us, riding these woods was as hard as trying to ride a horse underwater. So..."

"So what?" snarled Red. "Get to the point, you crazy fucker. Tired of hiding out amongst the willows today."

"So I weakened 'em. Right in front of everyone. I've been walking around, putting my initials on everything for a long time now. Long, long time. I figure one day if I can't ride the sheriff's best horses out through trees that thick, maybe I could ride those horses out through 'em instead."

"Ain't no sheriff in this town," Red muttered. "Never was and never is again."

"But there's water, boss," Little Joe says.

"Where?"

"Everywhere. How the fuck else can there be trees, goddammit. Those wells ain't dry!"

"Show me some water then," Red says.

"I'm showing you trees!"

"These trees are dead," Red laughs. "Haven't you been listening to the mastermind here?"

"It would have worked," Egg says, still going on about his plan. "Gray would never follow me through those trees. Back when they were alive anyway. I can push down any tree I weakened, any time I want. No one else can do it. Well, maybe one or two, but I have the only complete map up here in my head." He taps his temple for emphasis. "Gray would have never risked one of his prize horses to follow me, *especially* the white one. There'd be nothing but broken legs and broken necks as soon as they hit a tree that was still alive."

"See?" Little Joe points. "Trees."

"That's a horse, dumb ass," Red laughs, and they all turn as he jumps up to meet the white Palomino, a blaze of mustard and white visible through the scarred trunks.

"There you are, you dead bastard!" Red shouts as he runs. "Ha! Look at this goddamn thing! The beast has got sand, that's fo' sure. Horse has a fucking bullet hole through its head, but it still wanders back to where it was born if you forget to tie it down!"

He runs a hand through its yellow mane.

"Bullet in your head, but nobody told you," Red says with something like respect, then he grabs the horse's bridle, and it turns to look through him with the glassy yolk of its eye. There's dried blood around its muzzle, flies orbiting the hole where Red had plugged it. He starts to lead it around a short circle, then stops to look up into the trees. Jackass feels his nervous stomach squeeze, and he opens another bottle of whiskey to quiet it down.

"What is it?" he asks.

Red doesn't answer, just mounts the horse in silence, turning it to face the densest part of the woods.

"Boss, what are you doing?" Jackass sighs between swigs, catching on to the plan. "You don't wanna do that. You don't wanna weave that otherworldly, undertook beast through there do you? Let's just go around. This place is dangerous, creaking way too much. Egg, what did you do?"

"Any of you see that boy?" Red asks, nodding high, strangely thoughtful.

"What boy?" half of them ask back. The other half looking up and around.

"That boy. Up in the trees, saphead."

"You mean that dog we didn't see?" Jackass asks. "You told me I didn't see it, remember? Wait, what are you doing?"

Red heels the horse to get it moving.

"Got a dumb idea," he says.

"Dogs don't climb trees," Jackass explains to his bottle. "That the whole point of them things."

Egg runs past him and catches up with Red, eyes smiling, mouth almost connecting in the back, like usual.

"Hold on. I know what you're up to," Egg says.

"Oh, yeah? What's that?"

"You like my idea, huh? You're gonna try it."

"My idea now."

"You want me to show you what trees you can ride through?"

"What?" Red asks, finally really noticing Egg grasping at his leg. "No. Shut your cave, son. Your idea was fucking loopy. My idea's way better. I'm gonna see how far a dead horse can run through some dead-ass trees."

"Match made in heaven," Jackass snickers, as Red kicks the horse hard, and it gallops past the men and crunches into the undergrowth. Ten more feet and it's heading fast for the first tree. A couple more kicks, and the dead horse is moving like any horse with somewhere important to go.

Time slows to a crawl in their whiskey-soaked brains as the animal lowers its head and crashes into the first tree, splintering it like a giant wishbone. The trunk around the horse's skull, raining wood on the ground behind him. The gang runs to follow, heavy arms flailing. The horse hits a second tree, its body curling and shivering as it buries its head into the bark. Red has to grab the horn to hang on, knowing full well the boys will give him shit about this transgression later. The second tree creaks and crackles like a bonfire, slowly tipping, too. Blood and spittle run down the horse's snout, and Red turns the horse again, kicking at its flanks even harder, thundering through the dead woods faster and faster and faster. They grind through some smaller Guajillos and leather-leafed Acacias, bending them over like corn. They divide the twin trunks of an Ironwood like legs, heading for a final tree, a Ponderosa Pine. There's plenty of green on its branches, and not a single initial, heart, or arrow carved into its truck. It's alive as Hell, and just as certainly their final destination.

Both heads down, Red and his dead horse plow into the last tree like a steam engine folding up against a cliff wall, a previously unstoppable force finding its immovable object. Both shudder, the horse's ribs buckling like an accordion. Then it snorts some suds, drops to one shivering knee as black blood foams around the boiling hole in its skull. Finally, everything falls.

Red jumps off just before the irrefutable thud, steps back, then stands over the animal a second or two, hat tipped as he nudges it with his boot.

"Dead again."

"That musta been the last one," slurs Jackass, running up, out of breath.

"It ain't," Little Joe says, coming up behind him, pointing back to McKenna's barn in the distance. "I know she's hiding some. There's still horses on the Wendler farm. You can bet that xanthie's got secrets."

"I don't know why you keep—"

"Look at the fucking trees!" he screams. "The green!"

"I saw a man turn green once," Eggs says, smiling. "Didn't mean he wasn't dead."

"I'm telling ya, I've heard 'em," Little Joe says. "At night, you can hear 'em all in there, everywhere. There's horses, and that's a fact."

"He's right," Jackass says."Wendler's wife is hiding horses. I heard them in her barn when you fools were looking under beds for money."

"At least five horses," Little Joe says.

"No, there ain't, scrub," Red says, looking toward the barn, too. He starts trotting.

"Is, too," Little Joe says, running with him. "At least five horses, like I said. And if she's got horses, she's got to have water..."

"Ain't none left," Red says, running faster.

"I'm telling ya—"

"No, I'm telling you," Red says, elbowing Little Joe in the jaw and putting a boot on his throat where he falls. "And if there is, there still ain't." He puts some weight on it, and Little Joe's eyes show he's ready to agree with whatever Red says next.

"So listen to what I'm saying to you," Red tells the submissive thing squirming under his foot. "There's no law in this town. Maybe this is because there's no water. But mostly because there's no horses. And if there's still horses in this town, in about five seconds, there ain't gonna' be no horses in this town. Get it?"

Red lifts his boot, and Little Joe stands up looking about a foot shorter.

"That's the problem around here," he tells them all as he walks on. "A town still thinks it's a town because it's got goddamn horses."

SEVENTEEN

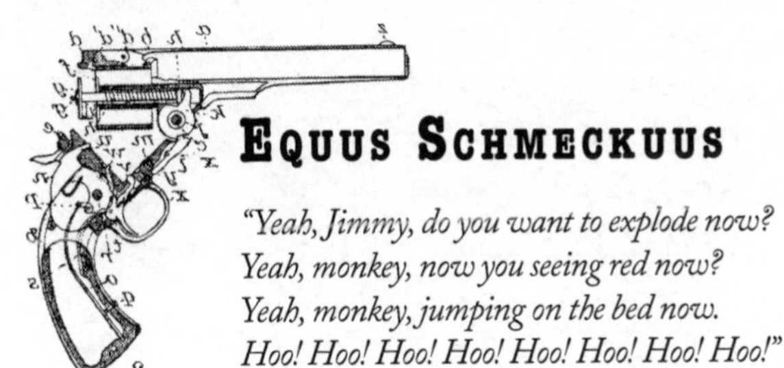

Equus Schmeckuus

"Yeah, Jimmy, do you want to explode now?
Yeah, monkey, now you seeing red now?
Yeah, monkey, jumping on the bed now.
Hoo! Hoo! Hoo! Hoo! Hoo! Hoo! Hoo! Hoo!"
–The White Stripes, "Jimmy The Exploder"

Red's dry eyes are burning so bad he thinks he can hear them sizzling in the afternoon sun. He closes them tight, counts to three in the shade of the double doors of McKenna's barn, then rips the lock off its hinges with one bloody, thorn-covered hand. Flinging the doors open, he steps inside as his gang runs past him to stand in the doorway, eyes smiling.

Five healthy horses snort and stomp, damp buckets and troughs of feed lining each pen. Jackass, Egg, and Little Joe shove each other to fight over the buckets, shaking and licking the last drips of moisture from the mash. The buckets fall from their hands when Red walks up to the nearest horse, pistol drawn, and the gunshot inside the barn ruptures three eardrums. The horse kicks a hole in the wall behind it, then collapses. The remaining animals scream in panic as Red's gang ducks down and huddles against the walls in shock.

Red moves to the next horse. Another shot echoes as it falls.

"Don't!" Jackass says, sobering up a bit, arms open wide from where he squats. "We need 'em! It's two weeks of desert in either direction."

Another shot, and another horse crashes to the dirt, hard-boiled eyes detonated, neck whiplashing in denial.

"See 'em drop?" Red yells. "That's what's supposed to happen when you shoot something in the head!"

Boom.

The fourth horse executed, Red clicks on an empty chamber while aiming at the eye of the fifth. As he reloads, Egg cautiously creeps closer, still staying low.

"Wait, wait," he says. "Please, wait."

Red looks to Little Joe to see what he thinks.

"Kill it," Little Joe says. "Why not?"

"Damn right why not," Red laughs. "Hell, I wish there was a goddamn unicorn in here so I could shoot that, too."

"A what?" asks Jackass.

"The ones with the wings," whispers Egg. "He'd do it, too. Then barbecue those wings."

Proud of his answer, Red steps forward to ruffle Little Joe's hair, and about a third of it comes out in his hand, fluttering to the ground like tinder. Then he cocks his pistol and moves it back to the fifth horse's eye.

He hesitates, taking a long look at the animal for the first time.

"Hey, is that…"

"Yep, that's the horse the Ranger rode in on," Egg says. "Black Mustang. Saw that shanny from a distance."

"Well, fuck him, too."

Click. Click. Red's gun is empty. He looks at the horse again.

"Naw, that ain't the same horse," Little Joe pouts, suddenly worried the last animal won't get shot. "I know that man, and I saw it, too. His Mustang was barely broke. And more blue than black. Snorting and bucking. I saw it knock him right to the ground. This one looks like it's holding its breath."

"Wouldn't you?" Red asks him, staring at the horse another ten, twenty, thirty seconds. Then he lowers his gun and strokes it, his thorny hand getting tangled in its mane. The horse is calm, big brown eye locked on Red. The Ranger's horse is impossibly calm, surrounded by such carnage and gun smoke. Its eyes are locked on Red's. To the gang, this stare down seems like love at first sight for both of them. Then the horse stomps a foot and snorts mucus onto Red's chest. He just laughs and reholsters his weapon. He whispers in the Mustang's ear, then backs up to lead it outside.

"Yeah, that's what I'll call you," he says to everyone.

"What did you just whisper to your black beauty?" Jackass asks, years past drunk. "Did I hear you say you named it 'Blue'?"

"Shut your cock holster. I said 'Blew.' I named him 'Blew.'"

"That's what I said. 'Blue.' Red and Blue! Match made in Hades."

"How are you spelling that?"

"How am I what?'

"Shut your yap."

Little Joe takes a bucket and walks through the cloud of gunpowder to position it under a dying horse's head. Thick blood trickles from the wound, then drips against the metal echoing like hammer strikes through all their ruined ears. Through these bucket taps, Red hears someone crunching around outside and turns to the double doors, and he turns to catch a glimpse of a young boy disappearing into the woods. Now he's nervous again.

"Was that the Wendler kid?" Red asks. "Can't be, right?"

"No way," Little Joe confirms. "I just left him in town."

"Was that boy running on all fours?"

"Huh?"

"Forget it."

Red shakes his head to forget what he saw, then leads the black Mustang out of the barn. He swings himself up onto the Ranger's saddle, and Little Joe climbs on and sits behind him, head against Red's broad back, his bucket of blood rattling in his hand. Egg shrugs, then climbs on, too, squeezing behind Little Joe, almost hanging over the horse's tail. Surprisingly, the Mustang tolerates all three of them, even turns to look down at Jackass like it's expecting him. Jackass shakes his head, almost knocking himself over from the effort, then pats the horse's neck.

"Thanks for asking, but I think I'll walk!" he announces. "That looks as high as me. And crowded. I'll just be dancing next to y'all!"

The men look off into the setting sun. Right then, a lone gunshot far in the distance.

"The hell was that?" Red says, turning the horse toward the

sound.

"Don't know."

"Church bell."

"Lightning!"

"Who the hell would be shooting beside us?" Red says, wrapping the reins around his fists. "Ain't nothing left around here to kill!"

The horse starts trotting when Little Joe tips the bucket back to drink. Coughing and gasping after a long draw of blood, he flashes a red-stained smile down at Jackass.

"Want some?" he croaks.

"Maybe later," Jackass says, walking heel to toe on an invisible log as he uncorks another of his endless bottles of whiskey. "Right now I'm on the lamb. Or dreaming of it."

This their third day without water, Red's gang turns to face the sun with no hope of catching it. Hidden behind them, a hunched Preacher leans against a dead tree covered in hearts to watch the four-headed shadow the cowboys have conjured on the horizon. He finds this likeness positively Apocalyptic. Then the Preacher sees the wobbly shape of Jackass stumbling beside the four-headed beast, tipping a bottle high and drunkenly weaving further and further away from the sun and the amazing mythological fusion of his former gang.

Three more tips of the bottle and he's walking alone.

EIGHTEEN

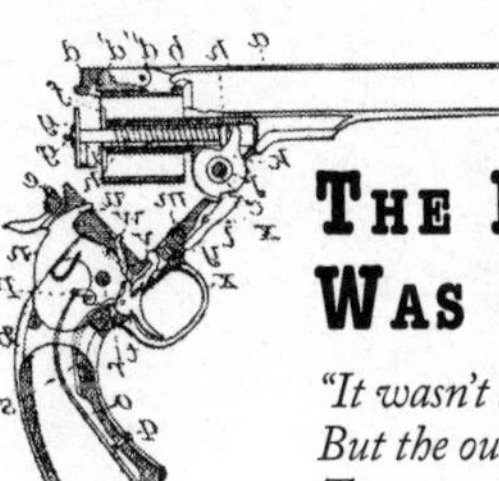

The Day the Electric Chair Was Invented

"It wasn't long before this story was relayed to Texas Red.
But the outlaw didn't worry, men that tried before were dead.
Twenty men had tried to take him. Twenty men had made a slip.
Twenty one would be the Ranger with the big iron on his hip."
-Marty Robbins, "Big Iron"

The Ranger is standing in the doorway of the barn as McKenna restrains Robby with an arm tight around his chest, struggling to keep him from running inside.

"How many?" McKenna asks through sobs, trying to keep her eyes from lingering on details of the slaughter.

"Four," the Ranger sighs. "But mine's missing. Of all the damn horses to save…"

"You can't still hate that horse when it's the last one in the world!" McKenna cries.

"Sure can," he says without conviction.

"But what about the deputy you came here with?" McKenna pleads, then to Robby, who's still fighting her grip, "Stop it! You aren't going in there! You're not going in there ever again."

"We can't wait for Tom," the Ranger says. "And we gotta *ride* outta here. We can't walk. You don't walk into a desert and back out again."

"But we don't need to go anywhere, Bob," McKenna says, then turns, thinking twice about what she's about to say.

The Ranger has her shoulders in his hands and spins her around. Robby takes the opportunity to break free and run inside.

"Tell me right now," the Ranger says.

"It was Gray. It was his idea. Gray filled those wells with sand. It was a trick to make people leave. There's still water everywhere."

"Goddamn that man. It's his fault daddy kicked you outta

town, too."

"Daddy never kicked me out. He threw me a wedding."

"A wedding has two people. Not one."

"Don't you mean three?" she says, looking down.

The Ranger lets her go, and they start to follow Robby inside the barn, then whirl around from a noise at the tree line. McKenna gasps, then buries her fist in her mouth to suppress a scream.

It's the Palomino. Gray's old horse. Red's new horse. At least it was Red's horse between the time he shot it then ran it headfirst into a tree. It emerges from the woods and into the light, one eye glued shut by scabs, its huffing nostrils streaked with ribbons of red and black, a crown of splinters ringing its muzzle, and a sunbeam shining straight through Red's bullet hole in its skull like a reptile's ear.

But in spite of these horrors, the Palomino still seems more alive than ever. The Ranger puts out a hand, and it walks up to nuzzle him, nose rooting in the salt of his sweat. The setting sun blinks through the bullet hole like the third eye of a fish, more like the third ear of a lizard. McKenna is sickened at first. Then she watches the Ranger's touch soften with the horse's breaths.

Robby comes back outside, hands bloody to his elbows. His jaw drops when he sees his father's horse, and he falls twice getting to it.

"Is that…?" McKenna puts her hand over Robby's mouth, fearing the horse hearing its name might break the spell and remind it of its dire condition.

The Ranger climbs on like his dad taught him once, and when he's up in the saddle, he holds his hand down for McKenna. She climbs up, too. Then Robby after her. The dead horse doesn't make a fuss, and this new, three-headed shadow of a family rides the last of the sunlight out of town. It's the steadiest ride the Ranger can remember, and he pats the impossible creature's head like an old friend. Or at least the dying horse of a dead friend.

"Not even when we were kids," McKenna says.

"What?" he says, looking up.

"I've never seen you do that."

"Me neither."

"I'd say it's good to see, but God help the kind of horses you'd love."

"True."

***

Agua Fría burns.

Propped up against a smoking porch, a dead undertaker grins from the sun-warped coffin he built the day before. The drunken last man on Main Street takes a long drink, steps high on a stack of pungs, and plays with the undertaker's jawbone like a puppeteer.

"'Hey, if I'm dead,'" Last Man says from the side of his mouth. "'Then who put me in this suit?!' Goddamn undertaker done got himself undertook!"

He animates the jaw a bit too frantic, and the bottom half of the undertaker's skull tears free like turkey meat.

"More like undercooked."

Then he takes the shard of an arrow from his coat and puts it behind the undertaker's head so it appears he was shot with it. The second-to-last man laughs, takes another drink, then wrestles the arrow away and jams it through the dead man's head. The arrow breaks off about a third of the way into the skull. A third man is so far gone he can do nothing but giggle at it all. None of them sees or hears the Preacher walk up, all black except for chipped teeth and the silver flash of a gun stuck in a belt pulled tight to its last notch. The gun is the only thing keeping his pants up.

"That's better," says Second-To-Last Man, stepping back for a better look. "What the hell were you trying to do? Not ruin the man? He was a good-lookin' rusher though, wasn't he?"

"No," Last Man says. "I was trying not to ruin my arrow. It's worth something. A gift from the... something-something tribe?"

"Oh, that kinda gift."

They all laugh together until the Preacher speaks over their shoulders, his voice rattling around his throat like coins.

"Is that supposed to be funny?" he asks the men.

"The world's ending!" Last Man shouts, arms out. "Everything's funny now."

"So, you *do* know the town is burning, don't you, boys? Who would have guessed a town that translates as 'Cold Water' would go up so easy?"

"We know it's burning," says Second-To-Last Man. "We're probably burning, too, just a little slower."

"Why didn't you leave when the water ran out?" the Preacher asks.

"Plenty to drink," says Second-To-Last Man, looking around for the bottle he dropped.

"And what's it to you, shave tail?" asks Third Man as the Preacher steps closer.

"Oh, I'm sorry," the Preacher sighs. "I guess you didn't recognize me without my collar. But I must ask, and I don't mean this to sound quite so threatening, but have y'all been to the glossary yet?"

"What collar?"

"Yeah, what collar?"

"I think it's gone black from the smoke."

The men twitch uneasily as the Preacher walks past them, long strides, tipping up a huge wide-brimmed hat and rubbing red eyes caked with ash from the burning storefront infernos on each side of the street. Then they shrug him off and go back to nursing their bottles, staring at each other as they suck away on the glass necks, until Last Man finally thinks of something to say and tries to clear his throat in preparation, hacking a spider of black mucus onto the top of his fist instead.

"You know how you always hear someone say, 'You wouldn't shoot me in the back, would ya, Billy?'" he finally manages to croak.

"Who says that?" asks Third Man. "I ain't never heard that."

"Any of you seen Red and his gang?" the Preacher asks. "Figured they'd be by, trying to drink up my Holy Water or something by now, but they ain't been around in awhile."

"Nope, sorry, Father."

"I'm not your father."

"Okay then," Last Man laughs. "Sorry, brother."

"Well, I suspect there's more for them to worry about than getting dry-gulched," the Preacher says. "In fact, I suspect that anybody left around here is about as dry as summer amadou. And so full of alcohol that a match and a bit of wind might be enough of a catalyst."

"Well, we're all that's left in this town," Last Man says, tapping the butt of his gun with a yellow fingernail. "Just us. Last ones standing."

"That may be true. But you should still be careful around an open flame, I would think," the Preacher smiles.

"Probably right," Last Man says. "You know what I was thinking the other day? Instead of hanging, they should invent something where you just light the poor bastard on fire. Maybe like a special chair or something where you just strike that match and *whoosh!*"

"Nah, too cruel," Second-To-Last Man says. "Takes too long to die."

"Not if you used lightning," Last Man says, forgetting about his gun. "I saw a man hit by lightning once, and he was dead *and* on fire, all at the same time. He coulda died nine times that way while another man choked and shit himself on the end of a rope. My idea ain't nearly as cruel as a hanging."

"And how the hell are you gonna get lightning to strike this special chair of yours?" Third Man asks.

"I don't know," Last Man sighs. "I heard there's really only three ways to die anyhow."

"If you don't count lack of water," says Third Man.

"More like a hundred and five," says the Preacher, pulling out a wooden match and striking it on the undertaker's coffin. All three men reach for their guns at the sound of the snap, then the hiss, but they're too drunk to stop laughing in spite of the peril.

"You wouldn't light a Christian on fire, would ya, Billy?" Last

Man snickers, and the Preacher flicks the match right at him in response. It thumps against Last Man's chest, and the other two hold their breath, expecting an impending detonation. There's a quick tongue of smoke and flame, then nothing. Everyone's giggling when a high-pitched crack rings through their teeth and eardrums, and a hole opens in their friend's chest where the match head was snuffed. He drops.

The last two men on Main Street try to stop laughing and turn to face the Preacher, now aiming his gun and grinning, as if preachers have always done things like this and today is any other Sunday. Their guns are out, but they're momentarily distracted by the Preacher's pants sliding off the knobs of his hip bones, and the Preacher quickly fires one, two, three more shots, blowing off teeth, chins, ears, smirks. Heads erupt in black blood and dust, all three men crumpling like money in a fist.

One man slumps into a rocking chair on the porch, and the fire from his burning body climbs the highest of them all.

"Have you ever heard of 'kenosis'?" he asks the dead. "Look it up when you get a chance."

The Preacher pulls his hat down to shield his eyes, then pries three more guns from the dead men's hands to tuck into his belt. Now they hold his pants up just fine.

***

Three miles down the road, Red and his boys ride the second-to-last horse in the world away from the black smoke staining the sky, passing a bucket of whiskey, blood, and thorns between their hands. An hour later, all three men are slumped forward, and the bucket falls with a clang when the Mustang stops to take a bright crimson piss.

An hour after that, the horse shakes them off like flies.

NINETEEN

Never Tempt Hate!

"Out on the corner with cast iron blood,
10,000 more with hearts on their own.
They say I might die, I may be cold.
I may have no Jesus, I may have no soul."
-Black Rebel Motorcycle Club, "Devil's Waitin'"

Night.

The Ranger, McKenna, and Robby are riding in silence through a ravine. Cliffs loom on both sides of them, pulling the sound from the valley and the air from their lungs. A figure approaches from the dark of their path, and the Ranger's hand sneaks near his gun as the shadow stops, then alters its walk to intercept them.

Finally catching the moonlight, McKenna recognizes the shadow as her former Sunday School teacher, with a half-empty bottle in his hand, three guns protruding from the front of his belt, and rolling eyes that seem quite insane. These eyes are locked on Robby, while the Ranger clocks the three guns. McKenna tries to break the tension.

"Hello, Preacher," she says, nervously. "Are you leaving, too?"

"How did you know who I was?" the Preacher says, amused, walking around to the tail end of the horse. "I'm not wearing my collar."

He stops to gaze up at Robby, now clutching his mother's waist.

"What's in your pocket, my son?"

"A rock shaped like a heart," Robby says, hugging his mother tighter. The Ranger swings a leg over the saddle to watch the man closer.

"No, no, that isn't a rock at all, is it?" the Preacher says sweetly. "You took the rock out of your pocket. What's in your pocket now?"

"Oh, yeah," Robby says, rooting around his shirt. "I forgot."

Robby pulls out the half of a Bible he traded earlier, and the Preacher makes a fast grab and comes away with one crumpled page. The Ranger watches close, holding his breath a second, surprised by the man's speed.

"Well, what you got there, boy?" the Preacher says, hacking a bit. "Don't be shy! Is that the first half or the second half of our Good Book?"

The Preacher studies the page he's snagged, then looks up and down the horse the family is riding. He walks around past the Ranger's legs to the horse's head, then wipes the hole behind its ear with a flapping page of scripture. The horse's blank, yellow eye never blinks.

"'*A pale horse...*'" the Preacher mutters.

Then he snaps out of his trance and looks up at the Ranger, who has assessed the threat and decided to signal his conclusions with a deep sigh. In the dark, the Ranger's eyes are almost as cloudy as the horse's, and the Preacher's hand drifts back to the hole in the animal's ruined cranium, seeming eager to explore the crater. The Ranger clears his throat, and the Preacher quickly brings the page up to his face and starts to read, coughing up his own dark saliva as a suitable prologue.

"'*Revelations 13... one of the heads of the beast seemed to have a fatal wound... but the fatal wound had been healed. So the whole world was astonished and followed the beast...*'"

He stops and looks up at them all, going from head to head, shaking his own slowly. Then he hands the crumpled page back to Robby.

"I once had a friend who got shot through a Bible he always kept in his vest pocket," the Preacher laughs. "Talk about tempting hate! Never tempt hate, boy. That's like wearing a bull's eye on your head. Or a Bible for a hat. Or riding three weeks into a town with no water."

"Don't you mean 'tempt fate'?"

The Preacher takes a deep breath then continues talking, slow, low, and serious.

"You know what happened to that man? The Bible stopped the bullet, sure, but it didn't save his life. The bullet was halted in its tracks by the Book of Job, which is precisely where they dug out the slug much later. But a piece of leather off the cover of that book skewered his heart, and it took him a month to die. And come to think of it, there were pieces of other passages, too, slicing up his heart muscles like whip cracks from some quirt. And as he expired, he prayed to the Lord to tell him what those pages meant. But he heard nothing. He was also shot seventeen more times, by multiple aggressors and multiple pistols, soon after the initial bullet."

"Interesting. Nothing more dangerous to bystanders than a barking spider," the Ranger says. "You know, I knew a man who took a bullet in the Bible once, too."

"Did you, now?"

"Yep. He had it in his shirt pocket just like you'd expect. And it stopped a .22 slug from finding a home in his heart."

"Well, he's a luckier man than my friend."

"Not exactly. A shotgun cut him in half before the .22. And that bullet in his Bible was later found to be from his own gun, as he tried to stop his own suffering."

"I like the way you grumble, sir," the Preacher says.

"Whose guns are you carrying?" the Ranger asks.

"Oh, these old things? No, not mine, my good man. One is for the moon, one is for the sun, and one is for… someone else. I already gave the sun his though," the Preacher says, pointing up. "Sorry if you were in the middle of reading your Bible earlier, but it only took one bullet to turn out the lights. Maybe you noticed?"

"You made it nighttime?" Robby asks, and the Preacher seems to notice him again, like he's never seen a child before. McKenna claps her small hands to get his attention back on the adults. Her palms are still shaky.

"Just so you know, Preacher, I knew it was you because you

are wearing a white collar. It's just so dirty that you can't see it anymore."

The Preacher cocks his head, curious, and reaches up to his neck to find the stained collar tight against his throat just as she predicted. Surprised, he squeezes it tight in his fist and rips it loose. He throws it to the ground, furiously rubbing his face and grinding the heels of his hands into his head. The tears filling the corners of his eyes are the only signs of dampness they can discern on his entire body, and these tears now stand out like open wounds.

"It's so, so hard to aim at the sun, you know?" the Preacher sighs, eyes pinched tight. "You have to look a long time right into that inferno before you can squeeze the trigger. And even if you *can* do that, you will eventually focus, and you'll see that fire for the first time. And you'll see that in the middle of all that fire and glare, the hot, yellow pain, you'll see that our sun is a lot smaller than you ever thought. Can you live with that knowledge?"

When the Preacher takes his hands from his eyes and looks up, the Ranger, McKenna, Robby, and the dead horse have moved on, only Robby still watching him from the tail.

The Preacher walks on, too.

And as he leaves the canyon and the last family behind, he comes to a clearing with rows of shadows that, at first sight, resemble flourishing crops in a farmer's field, and his stomach flips in anticipation. He picks up his pace even more when he sees a gate with the remnants of a stone wall on either side, long since crumbled, a sign looming above it. It reads:

"**SAN SIDRO CEMETERY**."

He walks through the tangle of headstones and thickets, weaving through the crude monuments, unreadable names, the dangerously leaning crosses. His hands move through a dead thorn bush, and he relishes the feeling of the claws cutting into the palms of his hands. But when he looks down, he's amazed to see deep slashes of white and no blood at all. He searches the sky until he finds the moon.

"So that's how it's gonna be, huh? Where you at now? That you up there, or are you hiding behind that white eyeball?"

He stares a minute, then tears off his loose shirt to leave it on a tomb like a ratty black flag. Consistent with everyone else in his doomed town, the dehydration has made the man smaller, swimming in his rags. But the Preacher feels stronger as he shrinks, truly believing he's actually getting younger, shriveling up back into a boy, back into his prime. He watches the moon as he undresses completely, relieved to see the moon does not shrink as the sun did earlier.

But he shoots it all night anyway, until it winks out forever.

TWENTY

The Day Drunk Driving Was Invented

"So he walked through the rain and he walked through the mud 'till he came to a place called The Bucket of Blood."
-Nick Cave, "Stagger Lee"

Night?

The Ranger, McKenna, and Robby are dying. They steer their dead horse in silence through the valley, hooves scraping through the stones that line a forgotten creek bed. When they round a cliff wall, the Palomino snorts, and Jackass suddenly yanks himself free from a shrub and lurches into their path. He stands nose to nose with the horse, both wavering like cattails in the breeze. A hint of orange from the burning town still pulses in the sky, and Jackass points an empty bottle towards it.

"Morning already?" he belches.

"Does he hear us?" McKenna whispers.

"Does he see us?" Robby whispers back.

The bottle slips from the drunk man's hand, and his feet cross each other a couple times to keep from tripping. Then he pulls two more bottles from each coat pocket and works on uncorking one with his last tooth.

"Doubt it," Jackass answers them as the bottle pops and he spins on his heel to take a drink.

"Did you say you were in mourning?" The Ranger asks, shaking the fog from his brain, then he pulls his gun and lines it up with the back of Jackass's head. He cocks the hammer, then changes his mind, lowering it. He holsters it and looks around, noticing the slant of a half-buried fence, a black stain on the ground where a cabin used to stand, and close to the path, a scrabble of chicken wire.

"Stay here," he tells the man, hesitating to shoot anyone who would likely soon represent the population of Agua Fría in its entirety. So he dismounts, steps up, and takes Jackass's gun before he can react, flinging it off into the dark towards the ruins of the cabin. He claps him hard on the back, dust exploding like a bomb of horseflies.

"Who the hell are you?" Jackass mumbles.

"The law," the Ranger says, then pulls him close by the collar. He sees this word means nothing to the man.

"You seen my deputy?" the Ranger asks. "Or his horse?"

"Did it have wings?" Jackass sincerely wonders.

"Been through a slogging? Drinking, too?"

"Maybe."

"You know it's dangerous to drink and ride, right?"

Jackass kicks some stones at a blood-rimmed bucket in the brush.

"I ran out of drink a while ago."

"Right," the Ranger says. "So what's in the bottles?"

"Water!"

"Like I said, too dangerous to ride in this condition."

"But I ain't on no horse."

"Yes, you are!" the Ranger barks, feeling a surge of strength at the idea of authoritarian duties. "Now step down off your animal and follow me."

Jackass drops one of his bottles, then the other. He blinks long, then shrugs.

"Okay," he says, swinging a leg wide out in front of him as if dismounting. He falls and collapses into a tangle of elbows and knees.

The Ranger waits for him to reassemble, then steps back in front of Jackass to scratch a long line in front of him with his boot.

"If you ain't corned... then walk that line."

"If I ain't what?"

"Heel to toe. All the way."

"What?"

"Walk the line, boy!"

Jackass looks down, then carefully plants his right foot and gives it a try. Confidence building, he tries his left. On his third step, he gets tangled and is back on the ground in a heap wondering how he got there.

"Who the hell are you?" he asks the Ranger.

"Told you already," the Ranger says, grabbing his collar again, this time pressing his gun flush against his chin. Rust flakes from the barrel smear Jackass's neck as he leads him to the chicken wire and shoves him face-down into the dirt. The Ranger looks around a second, then drags the end of the wire until it forms a half-circle around them both.

"You're too drunk to ride," he tells him. "Could kill somebody in a stew like that. You're gonna spend the night in jail. Sober up and you can rejoin the human race."

Jackass jumps back to his feet, bottom jaw jutting, ready to fight. But he hesitates at the edge of the makeshift chicken coop, stepping back again. In spite of the wire only reaching his knees, something in the Ranger's voice convinces him that he really is locked inside some kind of cell. He sits down again, slumps in despair.

"I wasn't on no horse," he's muttering. "No goddamn horses left… if there ain't no town, ain't no horses… don't know what the hell you think you're riding… saw that thing die…"

Then Jackass seems to understand his predicament for a lucid second, but not enough to understand he can step on out.

"Hey, you can't keep me in here!" he shouts. "I'll be dead by yesterday! Freezing out here… been raining for days…"

"Raining?" Robby asks.

"It's the thirst. Makes him see things that ain't there," the Ranger explains to them as he swings himself back up into the saddle.

They ride past Jackass, still mumbling in his impenetrable

chicken coop prison. Eventually, the mumbles turn to screams.

"Y'all'll be dead in a day!" he coughs "You lock me in here, but it don't matter! The same water that ain't in here, ain't out there neither!"

He squints at his bottles in the sand, outside of the coop, and he bares his tooth.

"At least leave me my rations! Let me out of here, goddamn it! I didn't do nothing! That man on the toilet was already dead! I can prove it! You can shit when you're dead. Tell the judge."

"You tell him," the Ranger says, as his dead horse disappears into the dark. "He'll probably be along shortly."

Jackass puts his head between his knees to stop the spins, still convinced he's locked in a cell for the rest of his life. He's half right.

***

Hours later.

Jackass hears twigs snap and turns to face a shape approaching from the black. He tries to stretch a grin across his tooth to seem friendly and winces from the pain of his split lips.

"Hey! Who's that?" Jackass asks, then he stops grinning as the shadow gets closer. It's a boy, the same boy his gang caught glimpses of before. The boy steps closer and stops at the edge of the circle of wire, eyes glowing to reflect the last of the blood-red fires in the distance, the smile on his face revealing seemingly hundreds of teeth. Sharp teeth. Baby teeth. Shark's teeth. Playfully, the toothy boy gets down on all fours and creeps slowly towards him, and Jackass's face relaxes a bit.

Then Jackass's expression contorts as recognition floods his face. In his drunken daze, he no longer sees a boy, but instead watches a snarling dog, an impossible dog with the rotting head of a shark fetus Jackass once saw in a bottle at a traveling Freak Show when he was a boy. The shark thing is lowering its head and stretching its neck, ready to lunge. Instead of screaming, he tries to coax the kid back from wherever he went to take the creature's place in this world again.

"Hey, boy, quit foolin'," he giggles. "You don't see a key out there anywhere, do ya?"

Then the shadow's closer, its own smile bloody and cracked at the corners, revealing more teeth than Jackass believed the world could contain. The monstrous shadow boy gets down on all fours and creeps towards him, and Jackass still hopes against hope that he just wants to play. Even when it tip-toes over the chicken wire to climb in and share his invisible cell, black, slippery tail whiplashing in the excitement of its meal, he still waits for it to vanish from his imagination. Then Jackass's mouth twists like a snake under a boot as he finally sees the boy clearly for what he is, and the infinite teeth rip his scream out into the dust while it's still traveling up his throat.

The shadow speaks.

"Sorry, I guess you didn't recognize me."

TWENTY ONE

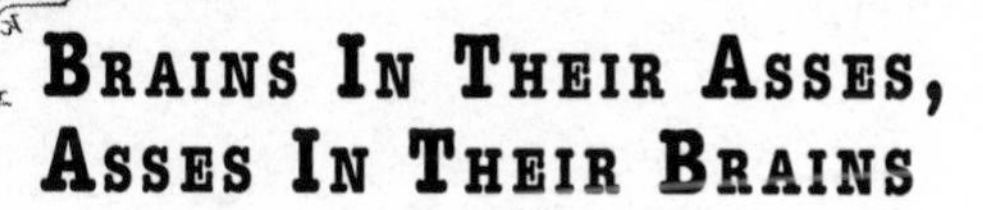

Brains In Their Asses, Asses In Their Brains

"Have you come here for forgiveness?
Have you come to raise the dead?
Have you come here to play Jesus
to the leper in your head?"
-U2, "One"

"Are we dead?"

Red, Egg and Little Joe are sitting with their backs around a tree trunk, empty bottles like rotten apples all around them. The Mustang is licking whiskey from a bottle and Red is balancing up in the air between his boot tips.

"Where's Jackass?"

"Don't know. Lost him somewhere back there. Where's Mud?"

"He'll be all right, men." Red reassures everyone. "Dead like us soon enough."

"I don't think we're dead," Egg says.

"Why's that?"

"Did y'all know that a Camel Spider can live for three months without water?" Egg explains.

"Dummy, you're thinking of a cockroach. A cockroach can live three months without food but only one month without water."

"No, Joe," Red says. "Now that's Egg you're thinking of!"

"Naw, Egg can only live a month without his head."

"We could test it! I probably could, too, come to think of it," Red says, doing the math in his head. "That's 29 more days than I need, tangle-footed or not."

"And you know what else?" Joe goes on. "A roach has a brain in its ass. That's why it runs so fast. In fact, I hear it starts running before its head even knows why it's running. That's why it don't need its head."

"Stop talking about my horse," Red says. "He's tired of the slander."

"See, you and me, boss, we're different. That's why we're gonna outlast 'em all."

"Did you just say you had brains in your asses?" Egg asks.

"No! Asses in our brains!"

"My mistake."

An hour passes. Then a day. Red stands up.

"Egg, you got enough spit left to whistle?"

"Yeah. Why?"

"What about you?"

"I do," Joe says, mouth crawling around his face as he makes sure.

"Good. I want you boys to do one last thing for me."

TWENTY
TWO

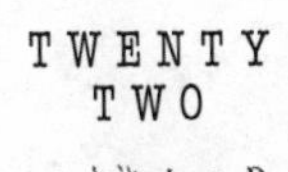

Three Ways Without Water

"It should be awhile before I see Dr. Death,
but it would sure be nice if I could catch my breath."
-Johnny Cash, "Like The 309"

Agua Fría border. Night.

The Ranger, McKenna, and Robby are still dying, but getting used to it as they stop at the edge of the open desert. Nearby is the smoldering fire pit of dead horses that the Ranger and Tom encountered on their way in. Three black vultures are perched on the charred legs.

"Three days without water is the limit," Robby reminds them, as if they need this knowledge.

"There are more ways to die than lack of water," the Ranger says, as if this offers comfort.

"Is that edible?" Robby asks, pointing to the fire.

"Only thing eatable over there are them birds," the Ranger says, taking aim with his pistol. He looks at his shaking hand and reconsiders the shot. They ride on.

"Sir, why did they call him 'Red'?" Robby asks after a while.

"Don't be tendsome, goddammit," the Ranger says, then apologizes for his demeanor. "I'm sorry, son. All right, I'll tell you why if you can tell me the name of this horse."

Robby shakes his head.

"I don't know. No one names their horses anymore, mister. Did you name your horses? My daddy said naming your horse is kinda like naming your feet."

"They called him Red because of his hair," McKenna tells her son.

"But it's not red, Ma. It's kind of orange."

"It's as red as hair gets," she says. "Everyone with orange hair gets called 'Red.' Or a 'ranger.'"

"Ranger? Like him?"

"No, 'ranger,' like short for 'orangutan.'"

"Orangutanger!" Robby laughs.

"That's not why he's called 'Red,'" the Ranger says. "It's 'cause..."

"I'm sorry, Bob," McKenna stops him. "But is this gonna be some story you tell me about him as a kid and I feel guilty for all the horrible sins and crimes he's inflicted on me and everyone else in this town?"

The Ranger stops his story, not confident it wouldn't.

They keep riding, Robby hanging lower and lower over the horse's tail, trying to hum a tune but weak from the hammer of the desert sun. He strains to pull himself up as he notices a dead animal in the wagon tracks behind them.

"What is it?" McKenna asks weakly.

"Nothing anymore," the Ranger says. "Things are gonna have to learn to stay off our trails. Gonna be more and more wheels every day."

"That'll be hard," McKenna mutters. "Animals usually want to take the same paths as men."

"Who told you that?"

"Something I heard in church. He liked to say that a lot, before he started drinking Apache tiswin."

"Well, one day, you'll see something like this every fifty feet, and maybe one day after that we'll walk on dogs instead of roads," the Ranger nods, then turns to tell Robby without conviction, "Don't worry, boy, we're close. I swear."

"We're going in circles," Robby says, staring at the skeleton, wondering how anyone could restrain a dog that size with only the thin collar of a priest.

As they ride, they take turns sleeping with their chins against their chests. They don't realize that they all share the same dream, even with their enemy. It's a dream of Agua Fría twenty years ago. A nine-year-old Red is sitting on the bar drinking from a mug while a burly, red-haired man drinks from a bottle. The sound of a fight erupts from a card game in the back of the room, and gunshots ring out. The bartender ducks down as stray bullets fly. As Red watches, the red-haired man's whiskey bottle and skull both explode without warning and shower Red with glass, blood, bone, and gore. Little Red blinks as chunks of his father's brain drip from his nose, then he starts to laugh hysterically, dragging red streaks through his hair with his tiny fingers as if he's playing in the mud. The shaking bartender comes up from behind the bar to grab the child. Then he drops the blood-soaked boy in horror when he sees that he's laughing. Red falls for what seems an eternity, finally splashing down at the bottom of a well. Only when Red hits bottom does he finally start to cry.

"What the hell is so funny?"

They all wake up when the coyote skeleton speaks. Sometimes it's the bartender.

***

Edge of the desert. Still night, mercifully.

The Ranger, McKenna, and Robby approach the vast sea of jagged black rocks barely visible in the moonlight on the horizon. Hearing something, the dead horse slows its gait and turns. Another horse is approaching at a full gallop from out of the dark, miraculously avoiding broken ankles on the uncertain terrain. It's Egg and Little Joe on the Ranger's Mustang. Little Joe seems more alive than ever, making him something like half alive, comparably.

"Where do you think y'all going?" he asks.

"We're not going anywhere," the Ranger says. "We're already gone."

The Ranger marvels at the sure-footedness of the horse he always hated, while Egg looks around Little Joe to size up the family.

"How many people do you think you can get on a horse? Seems like the old days of one head per horse shadow are looooong gone. You reckon five people could ride without..."

"It's a problem of supply and demand, I would think," the Ranger says.

"And drinking horses like tongue oil," Egg says. "Get me a doctor!"

"Shut the fuck up, Egg," Little Joe says with an elbow. Then he nods back at the Ranger. "I asked you a question."

"And I answered it. How old are you, kid?"

"Why?"

"Because I'd guess you're somewhere atween ten and a hundred and ten."

"Someone wants to see you," Little Joe says, and they stare at each other awhile, both fingering their guns like girlfriends. But just when it seems they're going to draw, Robby pulls the gun-shaped rock from his pocket in a quick, fluid movement. Little Joe flinches as if smacked, then barks a laugh when he sees what Robby's pointing, and he takes his hand off his gun. That's when Robby flips the heart over so the pointed end is up and throws it hard and straight at Little Joe's head.

It hits him square in the face, so hard it almost disappears in the dry meat of his cheek, and Little Joe slumps and almost rolls out of his saddle. Egg grabs him to keep him steady, then puts two fingers in his mouth and whistles loud. Spooked, the dead horse blinks and snorts something horrible, shakes its head, and starts to run its new family back in the direction it came. Little Joe and Egg follow on the Mustang.

But the dead horse picks up speed, still running back towards town, with the Mustang fast on its tail. The Ranger tries to stop the animal, kicking it hard in the ribs, but he gets no response. Right as the Ranger starts to panic and consider dumping everyone off the side, the animal suddenly veers and takes them towards the dense row of nearby trees. McKenna screams, and Robby covers his face with his arm as the dead horse crashes headfirst through one tree. Then another. Then another. The trees are hollow and brittle, long dead or devoured by insects, and the soft guts of them billow behind them as it runs and runs. Blood and spittle flies from the sides of the horse's mouth, a long string whipping them all about the face and head. The Mustang works to follow through the trees, but stumbles on a busted stump and pitches forward, spilling Egg and a semi-conscious Little Joe onto the ground.

And the dead horse keeps going. It crashes on through the brush, taking the Ranger and its new family through at least a dozen dead trees and finally to safety on the other side of the patch. There, it finally stops, nose bubbling black, and it walks in a slow circle like a clock winding down. The Ranger jumps off, pulling McKenna and Robby off with him. They step back and watch as the horse collapses hard in the dust, chest rising and falling like a pierced fireplace billows. The Ranger coughs, trying to catch his own breath, and McKenna checks her son's head and neck for injuries. Staring at the horse on the ground, the Ranger clears his throat to speak when a train whistle shrieks in the distance. New hope flashes on all three faces.

"Look! Smoke!" Robby points. Wafting over the top of a hill, a curl of black and gray is visible in the moonlight. They all watch as the wisp of smoke traces a line towards them. Then the train slows, stops, and backs up, chugging along back to where it started, finally disappearing behind a bigger hill on the horizon.

"Where'd it go?" McKenna asks.

"Don't worry about it," the Ranger says. "I never saw no train tracks around here. That was nothing that could have helped us."

"If that wasn't a train, then what was it?"

"I don't know. Another fire, maybe."

"I saw it!" Robby yells.

"Just another fire," the Ranger says. "Fires everywhere now."

"Fires don't move."

"Sure they do. Now they do. Whoever said fires don't move?"

"Then who whistled?" Robby stomps a foot.

"No one, goddamn it! There's no spit left in this world for whistling. And that smoke was just someone running around with their head ablaze. A burning head full of bad ideas, that's all that was. And he turned around and went the other way when he forgot his hat!"

McKenna and Robby look at him a second, then start laughing. Then he's laughing, too, since it's something to do.

"What the hell is so funny?" he asks, and they stop laughing eventually, not quite remembering the coyote bartender from their dreams, not sure why those words make their stomachs flip so suddenly. The Ranger walks over to the horse on the ground, reaching for a canteen under its leg. Water drains from a split in its side, and the dirt hungrily soaks it in. He throws it down, and McKenna retrieves it.

"Why aren't you drinking that?" she asks, horrified. "Why were you hiding it?"

"Because we never needed it," the Ranger says. "Come on. We're going back. Hell, it looks like we live here now."

TWENTY THREE

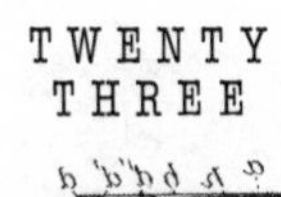

Eggbound and Down

"He's gone crazy, completely crazy,
trying to tame the American horse."
-The Cult, "American Horse"

Agua Fría.

Red is stomping through the black rubble of the church, sometimes looking for something important, like it's life or death, sometimes just kicking things to watch them jump. He pulls a chunk of smoking wood from the pile and throws it to one side. He digs into the soot, then spits black tar onto the broken cross that crashed down from the steeple minutes earlier. Satisfied, he looks up to see Little Joe and Egg riding toward him on the Mustang. Little Joe is slumped forward, a starfish of dried blood on his forehead framing a deep, dark gash.

"You kill that horse again for me?" he asks before he really noticed Little Joe's dire condition. "Hell happened to him?"

Egg climbs down off the Mustang, carefully bringing Little Joe down to the ground with him.

"I don't know. Happened too fast. I think he got shot? With a rock."

Egg leans back on his elbows in the dust and breathes deep. He reaches into his pocket and pulls out a big leather canteen and shakes nothing out into the dirt. Red watches him, watching Egg watching what he assumes is his beloved but fanciful spider. He watches Egg's eyes follow nothing as it skitters back to the shadow of his leg, and he runs a finger over this nothing, breathing a little easier. In spite of the legs of his fabulous arachnid rearing up in a defensive posture, Egg feels this nonexistent creature trusts him more than any man in his life.

Then Red's boot stomps down hard on Egg's hands. Egg's inhale freezes, mouth open in shock.

"Sorry, Egg. Got sick of that shit."

Red slowly picks up his boot, and his eyes widen when he sees the spider running away.

"Holy hell," Red whispers. Then Egg's hands are on Red's throat, and they both tumble to the ground. Red is so startled by the ferocity of Egg that he can't stop the assault at first. Egg is pummeling Red's face so fast he's able to land about ten solid shots to Red's nose before Red can finally throw him off to the side. Red goes for his gun, but Egg's on him again, furiously hammering at his mouth, one good punch sinking into his throat and almost stopping Red's heart. Red is so amazed by Egg's hate-fueled strength that he begins to cover up from the deluge of fists and try rolling away.

"There's water here, ain't there!" Egg hollers between punches.

"No!" Red shouts, face huffing dirt. "Gray was dumping sand in the wells! I saw him do it!"

"Bullshit!" Egg says, punching harder, afraid to stop. "That would take years to finish!"

"It's true. I swear," Red says, coughing up a thread of blood and snot. "At first I thought he was diggin' for something. But he filled all the wells…"

Egg tires a bit, and his punches slow down. Red spits more blood in the dirt, laughing and singing a song he first heard from a drunk uncle, whose primary existence was to teach their nephews drunken, slurry songs.

"*Egg-suckin' dog… I'm gonna stomp your head in the ground… if you don't stay out of my hen house… you dirty old egg-suckin' hound…*"

Then he rolls over to face Egg and holds up a hand. Egg pauses with a fist in the sky, cocked for another flurry.

"At first I thought he was digging," Red says mid-trounce. "But he was *burying* instead. Burying the *water*. I still don't know why.

Shit don't matter anymore anyhow."

Egg stops throwing blows and cracks his fist open, wheezing. His head drops. Panting for air, he sits back off Red's chest and digs around in his coat pocket.

Red takes advantage of this reprieve to quickly pull his gun with his thorn-covered hand and blow a bullet hole through Egg's chest. Egg rolls back off Red, both of his hands coming up to cover his mouth, like he's stifling a scream with a fist. Then he falls, arms limp like strings, his mouth working like he's trying for some important last words. Red is quickly sitting on his chicken chest now, his gun flush against Egg's cheek. He turns his ear towards him.

"What was that? Can't hear ya."

Red leans in close, then sees his gun barrel moving back and forth with Egg's face. He realizes that Egg isn't trying to speak at all, that he's chewing on something.

"What are you eating? It that a map?" he laughs. "Egg, are you eating the answer to everything?"

With a last surge of power, Egg spits a mouthful of eggshells and fluid into Red's wide grin, spattering the cuts on his bloody, ravaged face with foam and venom. Red jumps up and stumbles backwards, sputtering and wiping hard at his mouth and nose. He fans the hammer on his pistol and unloads the rest of his bullets into Egg's body.

"Goddamn you! Tryin' to poison me? Me!"

Red furiously scratches at the blood, spit, and eggshells on his face. Wincing in pain, he looks down to see his hand now carrying more thorns than his holster. He shakes some of them out of his skin, jams his gun back in tight, and screams at the sky.

"Who the fuck keeps doing that?"

Then he rubs his bloody palms on his thighs, blinking and circling Egg's corpse slow, staggering a bit, still laughing. Always laughing.

"Did you really poison me, you eggbound bastard? Or am I drunk? I can't tell."

He hears movement behind him and spins to draw his gun again, grimacing at the tangle of thorns. He sees his dead horse standing tall on the horizon, and he savagely rubs more blood from his eyes to make sure it's really there. But when he looks again, the Palomino has disappeared and instead he sees the Mustang on its side, dying. He sits down and starts plucking thorns from his skin.

"He loves me… he loves me not… he loves me not… he loves me not…"

TWENTY FOUR

Pricking Against the Kicks

"I was born to bring trouble to wherever I'm at.
Got the number thirteen tattooed on my neck.
They just gave me the number when I was young."
-Danzig, "Thirteen"

Desert. Night.

The last citizen to vacate Agua Fría is crawling on the ground, entering the brutal border of black, jagged rocks that circles the town like a coral reef. This particular resident is on all fours, which has become more and more common these days. From a distance it's impossible to tell if this shadow is man, woman, child, adult or some new amalgamation of horrors. But a lightning flash illuminates the sky and reveals it's actually a dog after all. Strong, healthy shoulders and sharp withers flex and roll as the canine scales the rocks, heading into the desert wastelands without any hesitation.

Another flash of lightning teases rain that'll never come, and the dog looks up to the sky, its black eyes burning with an anger only reserved for man.

***

Agua Fría. Church rubble. Same night.

"…he loves me not… he loves me not… he loves me not…"

Red is back to kicking through the ruins, like a huge toddler desperate for his feet to find a mud puddle, still occasionally pulling the thorns from his holster and his hand when he remembers them. Little Joe lies dying in the dirt nearby.

"I think I need water, boss," Little Joe says, barely audible.

"There ain't no water, son," Red says. "More important, am I growing thorns?"

"No, horns."

"How can I be covered in thorns if there's no water? That ain't how thorns work."

Red flips over a black chunk of wood with his toe, finds nothing, moves on to another.

"You need some comfort?" Red says. "Is that it? Okay. What if I told you I'm your daddy? Would that help you forget about water? I'm everybody's daddy. Maybe that's why I gave you all the numbers. You listening, you gone coon? You are my thirteenth son. Feel better? Let me know if you need any advice. Ain't got much time..."

"Liar," Little Joe says, eyes closed. "You lie about everything. There's water and you know it. Hell, you *said* it. You lied to all of us. Just some game you're playing with our lives."

"Maybe it's a game, but I'm playing, too," Red says, kneeling down in front of Little Joe. "I'm sorry, boy. I can't give you no water. If I did that, then it's like I never did anything. If I give you the water, then we didn't really stay in a town without it. Shhh... shhh... you see what I'm wabblin' here? If I give you the water, it's like I was here for the end of the world and I never did nothing at all."

Red sits and leans back on an elbow and watches the last member of his gang die. It only takes another minute.

"Wabblin' is dangerous business, huh, friend? In some places, it gets you killed."

When Little Joe's head drops to the side, he stands back up and starts kicking around the smoking pile of church rubble again. After an hour, he finally finds what he's looking for and claps his hands in excitement. He collapses back into the ruins, giddy, relieved, laughing at the sky.

"Can you believe that shit? I almost thanked you just now!"

He turns to Little Joe's corpse.

"You were wrong about one thing, son. Yes, there's water, but I pledge I ain't been drinking it. I played the same game you all did. This I swear to you."

***

Wendler farm. Night.

The Ranger pantomimes taking a long, deep drink of water and hands the empty tin cup to Robby, nodding in agreement.

"Yes, you were fast, son. You got any more of those magic rocks?"

"I got more rocks than anyone," Robby says, pretending to drink, too, energized by this action alone, swallowing air as fulfilling as any flood, feeling his body process the imaginary fluids, growing stronger by the second. He considers taking the Ranger to their well, Gray's hidden well, hidden well under the hay and horseshit, but then decides he doesn't need it anymore. He feels like a man, realizes manhood means dying, fast or slow. He studies his trigger finger.

"You'll find a rock shaped like everything if you dig deep enough," he says.

"Is that so," the Ranger smiles. There's a knock at the door, and his smile drops. He gets up to check it out, hands shading his guns

It's Red. His mouth is cracked open at least three inches past the bloody corners of his mouth, baked into this ghastly grimace forever from the prairie sun.

"No, no, don't pull your gun, Ranger," he says, looking him up and down. "Well I'll be damned. You are a big whaler, ain't ya? No, no, don't say nothin'. I don't want to meet you yet! I want to meet you later."

"When then?"

Red's eyes dart around the room.

"Fucked if I know. What time is it? Any idea? Someone said there was a deadline once, back when there were clocks in this world. Supposed to be three days and we'd all be dead, but it feels like three years. You got any horses to drink around here?"

The Ranger watches him ramble, waiting for Red's fevered, disintegrating brain to come back to the moment. It does, and suddenly it's clear from the look in his eyes that Red has finally recognized the Ranger from their childhood, and he's come to finish something for good.

"Meet me where the town used to be, Bob," Red says. "Where the church used to be, I guess. Listen for the bell to ring when the sun comes up."

"A bell on a church that ain't there? Sounds complicated. Let's just do it now."

"No, you can talk to Tom soon enough."

The Ranger blinks, shocked to hear the name.

"You didn't know about him and me, did ya, Ranger?" Red says. "I mean, him and me before the other day? You should know that I paid that Judas steer a hundred bucks to bring you to town. My own personal mailman. My poster boy, you might say! Pretty sure he earned it. Though all that money weighed him down a bit."

The Ranger decides not to believe any of this right now, and Red walks off into the dark.

***

Dawn. Church ruins.

Red shoals in the rubble with Egg's headless corpse, a bloody axe leaning on his back like a friend. He has the church bell resting against a knee, and he's stroking the bell's pitted tin skin like a cat. Absent-minded, he pulls Egg's head close, too, and searches for the number of his brand. He realizes he destroyed it when he hacked the head free, so he scratches a new number into Egg's throat with a yellow fingernail.

"You know what?" he asks the head. "Everyone thinks that it was the whiskey that made me mean, even back in Bisbée when I first started wakin' them snakes." He taps Egg's cloudy eye for emphasis. "That just ain't true. The drink made me smarter, not meaner. That's why I was able to run this town. That's why I am the last man standing."

He stares at Egg's headless corpse a few seconds.

"Okay maybe not the last man standing, but I'm the last man planning!" Red works a finger into the socket to loosen some dirt that's gathered under the lid, but this just pushes the eyeball in further.

"You know, you were right, Egg. We don't really need our heads after all. At least *you* don't. You're way better without it." Red brushes his hair from his face, tearing away a handful by accident. "Look at you. Can't spit at me no more. And you can't keep filling my holster with thorns when I'm sleeping, you sneaky fucker. That was a good trick, by the way. And no more soaking my clothes in whiskey. What was that all about anyway? I truly think that's what's kept me alive, but I ain't no scientist. Must say, though, I think you did poison me today, and it didn't take your secret handshake to do it."

Red kicks at Egg's leg, watching the eyes on the severed head for any reaction, then he sighs.

"You really *don't* need your head, do you? I'm sorry it came to this, but I finally feel like I can talk to you. Did you know that when we was little, Bob Ford once whispered to me, when no one was around, that one day he'd love to have my head bottled like a jam jar? On a shelf like some butterfly, under glass with all his paw's weapons, named and numbered for all to see. Can you imagine such a thing? And *I* was the bad seed? Maybe it was his paw who said it, but who even considers loco shit like that? You tell me. You collected heads, didn't you, Egg?"

Red pulls the bell up onto his legs to share his lap with Egg, and takes out his gun to bang the barrel against the sides of both. Dark blood covers the skirt of the bell, and the sound of the gun on the metal is muffled, truncated with no echo at all. But the sound on Egg's skull is deafening. Red lifts the bell, peeking underneath, then covers Egg's head with it entirely, screwing the iron down around his split, cauliflower ears like a street thief readying his shell game. He lays his own ear against the side, laughing as he keeps banging.

"Egg, can you hear me in there? You're the only one who knows. What time is it now?"

TWENTY FIVE

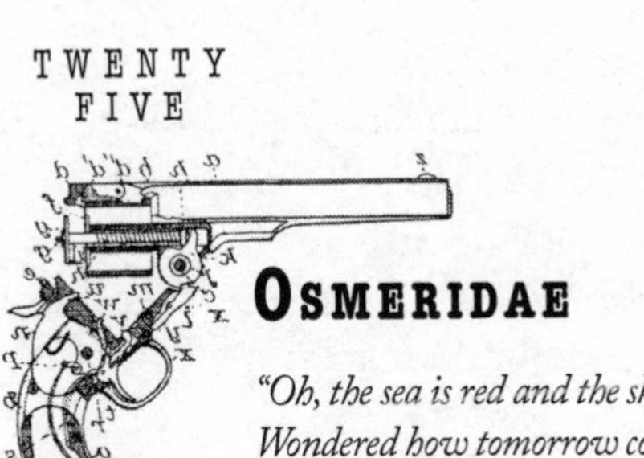

OSMERIDAE

"Oh, the sea is red and the sky is gray.
Wondered how tomorrow could ever follow today...
The mountains and the canyons started to tremble and shake.
Children of the sun begin to awake. Watch out!"
-Led Zeppelin, "Going to California"

Bisbée. Twenty years ago, at least.

A Future Ranger and his father are standing over a small, dust-and-rust covered revolver, still trying to find anything to fit the boy's little hand. Ready to give up, Sam blows some insect shells off the worst gun in his store.

"October. With the droughts, Smith & Wesson had just went bankrupt like everyone else. That was the year this gun was coming out. So they had to build this with spare parts and substandard metal. It's a .30 caliber piece of shit, and you shouldn't even be looking at it. You've got a one-in-ten chance of it exploding in your hand every time you fire it. That's why it's my Halloween special! For you. Trick or treat."

The Future Ranger never loses sight of the gray, featureless gun, continuing to glance back at it as they move down the line. His father's quick dismissal of the weapon makes it the most fascinating one by far. Sighing, Sam picks up a thin-barreled weapon to distract his son, a gun that closely resembles a toy he picked up from a snake oil salesman after the first of the brutal Arizona droughts. It looked real enough, minus the squeeze bulb.

"November. There's a good story with this one. Looks like that toy, don't it? You remember that Parker Stearns & Sutton USA Liquid Pistol you wanted so bad? I got suckered into buying that one cause they swore it could put out a fire. And there is something to be said about pointing a gun at some flames to make them go away, like the opposite of what you'd expect! Bullshit. It was the first thing to go once that fire started. But this gun only looks like a water pistol. Now, some say that Joe Wesson joined Smith & Wesson on November 11, 1880 at the age of 21. But I hear that's actually when him and Smith's youngest son had their first duel. And he was fast, too. He was so fast that, for awhile, the company was called Wesson & Smith! And this is the gun that boy used, because it looked like that toy, this crazy Luger-looking thing with a stripper clip you pulled to chamber the bullet. He called it the 'Blow Forward.' And I ask you, what kind of name is that for anything shaped like this?"

"But…"

"Wipe your chin and listen, son."

Sam takes his son's elbow and drags him down to the last gun on his counter.

"Finally! Your last hope! December. It was December, 1882 when Joe Wesson, D.B. Wesson's youngest son developed this. It's the .44 Hammerless, also called the .44 'Humorless' by the boys in his office, mostly called 'The New Departure' by the boys in the factory, a name that stuck with the public, too. And it's a good gun for December weather. No hammer to freeze and one extra trigger in case the first one locks up. See that? It has no hammer but two triggers. The lower trigger rotates the cylinder and cocks the invisible hammer inside. Look. Look here, I said!"

Sam holds the gun out to the young Ranger. He holds it carefully but struggles to get his hand around it. He can only squeeze the bottom trigger with his middle finger, as it just barely reaches the top one. Embarrassed, the boy hands it back.

"Did you take the hammer off this?"

"Why would I do that?"

"I don't know, Daddy. You did just lie about Smith shooting Wesson."

"So?" Sam says, smiling. "It's a good story ain't it? Leaves an impact."

He remembers when his father tried repairing guns for a living, before he resorted to sales, then finally to collecting. He ruined all the weapons he serviced, however, a reverse Midas touch, as his only training was based on a discarded Sears & Roebuck Co. catalog where all the "exploded" gun schematics had been printed in reverse.

"I don't know. Maybe I'll just take October."

He walks back down the line and reaches for the gray, lumpen revolver, and his father spins him around.

"Why the hell would you go for that? After looking at all these, you really want that? You don't want that."

"Tell me about it again. You said 'substandard metal.' What kind of metal did they use then?"

"Pig iron. Mixed alloy. Worst of all worlds. It looks like a rock for a reason, boy."

"How big?"

"How big what?" Sam asks.

"How big was the iron?"

"What the hell are you ... no, I said 'pig' iron, not 'big' iron, dummy."

Sam affectionately rubs his son's head in spite of his disgust, then cackles when he picks the gun back up.

"If that's what you want, fine. It's all yours, boy. Happy Halloween!"

"Daddy, how can these twelve guns be your calendar? There's years missing in between each of these guns. I don't get it."

"A man doesn't need to know what year it is. He just needs to know the month."

"But you thought it was March before. And now you're saying 'Happy Halloween.'"

Sam says nothing.

"So, I can have it?"

"I said you could, if you really want it. You realize they don't make them out of pig iron for a real good reason, right?"

"If I take it, how will you know when it's October?"

"Because I won't have a gun for a whole goddamn month!"

"Right!"

"Or a son."

"Right," the little Ranger agrees, not really getting the joke, and he claps his hands, trying to act like it doesn't hurt. "So, are we going to California like everyone else? I heard people talking about the wells running dry around here."

"Who was talking about that? No, no, no, that's five towns and nine years away. If it ever happens. The Arizona droughts are over for while. Nothing for you to worry about. Right now I want you to worry about *right now*."

"Does it work?" the tiny Ranger asks, staring at his new gun, cocky but doubtful.

"No. I already told you. You picked the worst one."

"But it's the only one I can carry," the Ranger says, skinny arms crossed, belligerent.

"Maybe it'll do," Sam says thoughtfully. "Who knows? The man who traded it in said to me, 'Metal has rock and rock has metal, so it doesn't matter what you're pointing at another man to threaten him. As long as it's not just your finger.'"

"What's that mean?"

"Hell if I know. Sounds like Indian bullshit."

"Does it have a name?" the Future Ranger asks, fingering the trigger and aiming it at insects in the corners.

"I called it 'Sioux.'"

"I don't know if I want a gun named 'Sue,'" he says, arm and weapon dropping.

"No, not 'Sue.'" Sam says. "I said 'Sioux.' Like that Indian bullshit we were talking about. That's the name of the squaw who swapped it. Them Sioux were always sayin' shit that didn't make much sense."

"Okay. I'll take it."

"As if you ever had a choice."

The young and Future Ranger puts the gun in his belt, and his pants are tight for the first time in his life. Then pulls it out fast and points it at the window, the door, then his dad, in succession. Sam shakes his head and sighs.

"Life ain't gonna be easy for a boy with a gun named 'Sioux.'"

***

Outside behind the gun store. Later that day.

"You ever heard the word 'smelt,' son?"

"Yeah. It's a method of extracting metal from iron ore by fire. It's how men make guns."

The once and Future Ranger stares at his father a moment, dangerously close to connecting over the symbolism of that term. Then his father shakes it off.

"Nope. It's a fish."

"Okay, it's a fish. So?"

"It's a little fish. Like you."

"How is it just like me?"

"Because that's a fish that everyone eats whole."

Sam is towering over the scene, blocking the sun, arms on his boy's arms, showing him how to hold the gun steady.

"Listen up. If you insist on playing this game, there's some rules," Sam says. "You listening?"

The Ranger squints down the barrel, the shake of the gun slowly steadying from the soothing voice of his father an inch from his ear.

"Rule number one... keep the sun at your back. Number two... maintain eye contact. Number three... keep your holster waxed. Number four... don't talk. Number five… shoot when *he* talks. Number six... always shoot for his buckle."

The Ranger's arms drop again.

"Now, why do I shoot for his buckle?"

"No idea. Quit wabblin' and don't ask questions."

"What day is it?"

"Man doesn't need to know the day. Or the year. Only the hour."

"What if he ain't wearing a buckle?"

"Then he's unarmed, and this shit ain't even happening."

"But..."

"Okay," Sam sighs. "You shoot for the belt buckle because with the adrenaline spike, aiming any higher will put the bullet over his head."

"And why do I shoot when he speaks?"

"Because when someone is talking, they won't know what hap—"

The boy pulls the trigger, and the gun explodes in his hand.

Past, present, or future, a gun will always explode in the Ranger's hand.

TWENTY SIX

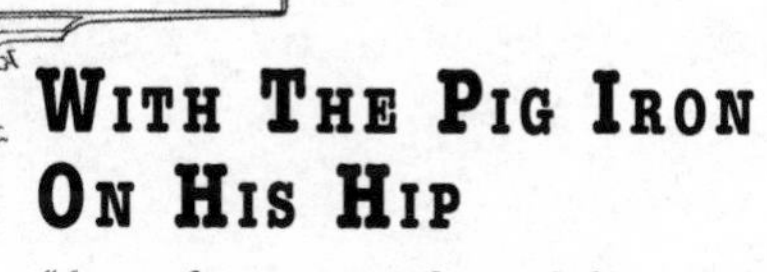

With The Pig Iron On His Hip

"An eye for an eye, and a tooth for a tooth.
And anyway I told the truth,
but I'm afraid I told a lie...
And I think my head is burning..."
-Nick Cave, "The Mercy Seat"

Agua Fría. Center of town. This very morning. 11:27 a.m.

The sun is risen, and the wind is roaring. Huge waves of sand lap at every smoking doorway and the burnt shell where proud structures used to stand.

The desert has reclaimed the town.

Red sits cross-legged in the middle of a black crater, still banging his gun against the scorched church bell resting on his knees. Something is coming toward him, a monstrous figure swimming through the sand and smoke, and Red stands and walks to the road to meet it, using his knuckles to try and rub some sense into his bloodshot vision. He sees a man in white, riding high on the clacking skeleton of a horse. Red grinds his poisoned, alcohol-fueled eyes hard enough to feel them sink into his skull a good half inch, and the man in white and his skeleton steed finally disappear. It's just the Ranger walking toward him through the heat and smoke shimmer, and Red's disappointment is obvious.

"Oh. You. Hot as Hades out here, ain't it? Hey, do you know what time it is?"

The Ranger says nothing, just keeps walking towards him.

"Do you know the hour?"

Still no answer from the lawman.

"Do you know the year?"

Nothing.

"Who are you? Do I know you? I know you!"

The Ranger stops about thirty feet down the road. Eyes dancing, Red grins wide, too wide, and a couple of his sharper teeth drop out of his mouth, but he doesn't blink. The Ranger finally speaks.

"It's October. That's all I know."

"Don't think so, Bob. It's too hot out for that."

"Maybe," the Ranger agrees.

"Are you here for Gray?"

"I'm here for my family."

"That was my family. You just don't even fuckin' know the score."

Red trails off, then motions to the empty road behind him.

"You know what? Me and my boys here were talking the other day, and we heard that to really be a man you're supposed to have killed the same number of men for every year that you've been alive. Have you heard this formula?"

"I have. For the most part it's true. Except you forgot the number of horses."

"Ha! I can't drink that many horses. But I'm 21 today. Or was it yesterday? How old are you?"

"53."

The crazy smile on Red's face finally drops and he does the math, and his expression for once shows true fear for the first time.

"What time is it?" Red asks again to buy some of that time back. "Where's that horse? You seen its eyes? Got the yellows. You got the yellows?"

"It ain't dawn, if that's what you were waiting for."

"Dawn. 'Noon? Playin' a tune? Same difference," Red says, squinting to the sun. "We're all the same roastineers." He looks down at the Ranger, ducking to get an angle under the man's hat.

"Why the silence? Why the stone face? Why is it the same with all you cocksuckers. Ain't it exhausting keeping that silent shit up?"

The Ranger just stares.

"I'll *tell* you why. Because the first time a cowboy claimed he was a cowboy was when he killed a man during a card game, when everyone in the world was wearing that stupid poker face under his hat. Ever since, it's required. Even with no cards in sight. Notice I can't shuffle my hands with cards like these."

He holds up his bloody, spiked palms, and the Ranger takes a long look.

"Is that crazy horseshit your last words then?"

A cloud covers the sun, giving them both a good look at each other, and Red looks back down the road and keeps talking, confidence back, waiting for an opening.

"October, huh? Halloween? You know how all that trick-or-treat stuff got started? All the candy for the kids? It all started with bobbing for apples. Except they used to shoot them in the barrels, not bite them. Maybe if we were still shooting those apples, people would still fight with their teeth."

Still nothing. Red pretends the Ranger responded, pretends his gang is still with him, too.

"What in the plaguily hell are you talking about? Hell if we know, right, boys?"

The Ranger tips his hat way back, and he's almost smiling.

"You talk a lot," he says. "You done?"

Red just keeps grinning, his tongue snaking up to explore the holes in his gums where his canines used to be. The remaining teeth around the gaps wiggle like cattails.

"It's really too bad 'cause I'll bet I can whistle like a bitch now. And those dead horses would just keep coming!"

Their muscles tense before the draw, but without Red seeing the motion, the Ranger's hand is suddenly up and aiming, but empty. A lone finger. Then a bullet hole opens in Red's chest like a flower bloom, then another in his throat, then one over his eye. Flames flicker around the hole in his chest, and the Ranger is amazed to see Red ignite. In a flash, Red's engulfed in flames and walking in a circle, mouth moving like a little fish that lost the water. Then he collapses.

The Ranger holsters his weapon, never knowing he was so fast Red couldn't see the gun, only the damage it had done. He walks closer to the burning man lying contorted on his side, one thorn-covered hand still scratching at his holster, his alcohol-soaked clothing burning like a brush fire, mouth still working as his tooth pulp popped like corn.

Through this conflagration, Red can still see something of his world, and the bullet holes on his own chest, neck, and throat shrinking and closing like dying bulbs. He sees the Ranger screwing his hat down tight over his eyes again, no gun in sight, still pointing his finger, just one finger to accuse him of every sin at once. High behind him, Red sees a boy sitting on a dead branch, the black leaves of the tree flashing red, then green, then black again. Then the leaves rustle and flutter from every limb in a dark explosion, a grand ovation, and Red tries to stand as the ruptures and the fluid in his burning lungs drown him in his own blood. The last thing Red sees as he falls back into his fire are four skeletal horses along the skyline in perfect formation.

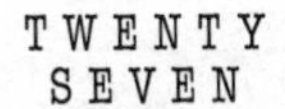
TWENTY SEVEN

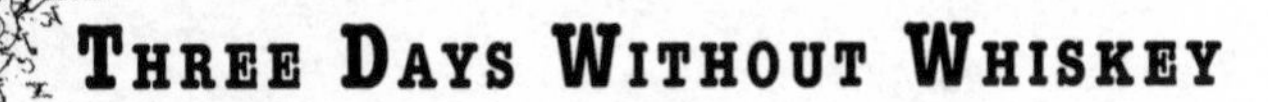
Three Days Without Whiskey

"There was twenty feet between them when they stopped to make their play.
And the swiftness of the Ranger is still talked about today.
Texas Red had not cleared leather when a bullet fairly ripped.
And the Ranger's aim was deadly, with the big iron on his hip..."
-Marty Robbins, "Big Iron"

Bisbée, New Mexico. Year indistinguishable. 12:09 p.m.

The Ranger is walking through the ring of weeds around his father's home. Though only a year has passed since the fires, he looks a hundred years old, his stone face a roadmap of wear and tear. He places a palm on the door of the store when a small boy turns the corner fast and almost runs into him. The boy looks up into the shadow under the hat, smiling and tossing a ripe, red apple back and forth between his hands.

"He ain't here," the boy says. "He's down the road. At Uncle Ron's."

"Your uncle's?"

"No, your uncle's."

Not that again, the Ranger thinks.

"Do you know me?" the Ranger asks, but the boy ignores the question.

"Did your father ever show you *his* father's gun? It was a big iron, that weapon. A one-off custom handgun chambered in .45 Colt but featuring a Great Western copy of the Colt Single Action Army frame, with a Colt 1860 Army backstrap, a grip frame, and a cut-down 9 and ½-inch Marlin rifle barrel. Fired once in anger then trigger-locked forever."

"You know a lot about guns, kid."

"I know a lot about lots of things. You know there's never been a tornado around here? Ever. Something about where this town sits between the mountains? Tornados is something that just doesn't happen to us."

"That so? Well, son, I remember hiding from tornados as a boy your age, many, many times."

"You were a boy my age many, many times?" the boy laughs. "Me, too!"

The Ranger cocks his head a bit, looking the kid over. He can't tell whether the boy's hair is red or just that loaded with desert sand and dust.

"You know," the Ranger says. "Maybe it was just an excuse to get the family together underground to play cards."

"Had to be."

"You know me or my family?" the Ranger asks again.

"I know you," the boy says. "Whole town knows all about you and the gunfight. And the fistfight. And the fires. Been a lot of talk about what actually happened there. Hey, where's your horse?"

"I don't use animals to get around," he says. "These days, a man shouldn't ride on anything alive."

"That why it took you a year to come home?"

The Ranger ponders this, always confused without a calendar.

"So, what do they say about me, boy? I didn't know there was anyone around to say anything."

"The gun fight or the fist fight? Well, some say Red never cleared leather, some say you never had a gun, some say you shot him with your finger, some say it was your very own son hiding in a tree that day who slayed Red from there. Some say he threw a rock, some say *you* threw a rock, some say a crazy Preacher shot him from the shadows and it lit him on fire…"

The Ranger leans back against his father's door and tips up his hat up to keep listening.

"…some say Red fired first, but the sparks ignited the whiskey in his body, some say it was the whiskey on his clothes, that he never drank at all, some say his own gang soaked him in whiskey while he slept but died of thirst before they could light him on fire themselves, some say it was going a year with whiskey, then three days without, that made him explode, some say Little Joe was really Red's son and he shot him from that tree, some say Joe was really one of Red's thirteen sons in three towns, and some say they saw a dog up in the tree that day, not that a dog can hold a gun... or climb a tree. And some say it was your first bullet that started the fire, or your finger, because the doctor told you that you only had a month left to live. But mostly I just tell everybody it was me."

"Naw, that story about my first bullet. Shot from my finger. Go with that one."

"Is that what happened?" the boy asks, deadly serious now.

"I honestly don't remember. I've been walking so long. I thought it was you."

The boy frowns and kicks at some stones, and the Ranger blinks at the dust circling the boy's shoes. For a second, his eyes are blurry, and he thinks the boy's fixing to ride a tiny cyclone up and over his head, straddling the whirlwind like an angry gray pony. Then the boy throws the apple up in the air and catches it and his eyes focus again.

"I'm surprised to find anyone here, kid. I thought this town was drying up, too."

"Ha ha! No, we got a school now and everything," the boy says proudly acting like it's funny "Not that I need it anymore. I've learned almost everything there is to learn."

"Really? How old are you, boy?"

"Can't you tell?"

"Not any more. How old do you think I am?"

"Two hundred and thirty-nine," the boy laughs, then stops. "No, wait, sorry. Two hundred and thirty-nine," he laughs again.

"Nope, my birthday ain't till tomorrow. So tell me, what's the last thing you learned in this new school of yours? Before you didn't need it anymore?"

"We learned about the first movie ever made! It was real boring though. Just a movie of a horse running. That's all you see. Nothing else, just a horse running about a hundred feet."

"What kind of movie is that?"

"If you'd listen, the man who made it wasn't trying to make a movie. He was just setting up this long line of cameras to watch a horse's legs so they could figure out how to train them better."

"Let me guess, they didn't figure out shit with those beasts."

"Well, they figured out movies!" the boy says, taking a big bite of apple. "And they saw for the first time that when a horse is running, all of its legs are off the ground at the same time. Turns out that, about half the time they're running, horses aren't really running. They're really *flying*."

The Ranger frowns as he thinks about this a moment.

"My father could never make it three days without whiskey," the Ranger says, almost to himself. Then to the boy, "Still not much of a movie."

"I think you're right. I think the first *real* movie was the next thing this man filmed. That's what we're learning right now. The first real movie was a series of pictures of one man throwing a bucket of water on another man. But, you know, that wasn't really a movie either."

"Was it a honey bucket?"

"Ewww! No, a regular bucket."

"And why isn't that the first movie?"

"Because the man getting splashed looked mad. Mad in real life."

The Ranger smiles at this, understanding what the boy means and thinking about his past year on the road and the family he lost somewhere along the way.

"So, what was all the fighting for?" the boy asks.

"Someone said there was gold in one of the wells. A rumor ran through the town like a brushfire."

"You know, I think that story started with me. Or my sister. That was our well. But it only had a penny in it."

"Your sister? Don't you mean mine?"

"Maybe. A penny is still gold though, right?"

"I guess you're right," the Ranger says, and the boy ponders this a minute, holding the apple in his mouth but not biting down. Then he spits, and the questions start rolling again.

"Hey, did you have a gun when you shot Red? Or was it really just a rock in your hand? Or was it just your hand in your hand? Which finger?"

"No, no, no. It was a gun. See?"

The Ranger reaches into his holster and surprises them both when he comes up with a long, sharp, pointed stone. He scratches his head under his hat.

"Wait," he says, seeming to lose another year while the boy watches. "I don't remember where. Long time ago, I traded that gun for this rock. I think. There was a boy on the road, a Dakota Sioux, and I needed a knife to cut some hides. And I traded him my gun, the gun my father gave me, for this sharp stone that his father gave him. I think."

Everything fades.

***

The world snaps back into focus.

The boy still stares at him, wide-eyed and blinking, and the Ranger backs up off his father's door.

"I'm sorry, kid. I haven't been able to remember much these days…" He trails off, looking at the rock, then to the boy. "How long you been there?"

"I just got here. Some kid traded me this rock."

"That's my rock," the Ranger says, baffled. "Did I give you that?"

"Nope. Like I said, some kid did. I just got here. Ain't you cold dressed like that?"

The Ranger studies the sky, tries to guess the season, realizes it will always be impossible.

"You want it back?" the boy asks.

"Keep it."

"It ain't mine," the boy says.

"Sure it is. You want it anyway?"

"Yeah!" the boy shrugs, turning it over and over in his hands. "What's it made of?"

"It's more rock than metal really. Same metal as my gun. Steel, iron ore, coke, limestone, carbon, hydrogen, oxygen..."

"Hey! That's water! And we're water! We learned that in school, too. So, we're made of the same thing as a gun?"

"No, the same thing as a rock," the Ranger says, walking away. "Turns out, we don't really need water at all."

"No, sir, I heard that people are made out of mostly water."

"Nope. We're just blood, rocks, shit, piss, and hate."

"And water."

"Do me a favor," the Ranger says, turning back to the boy. "Spit on the ground for me."

"Why?"

"Do it. I want to see something."

The boy does what he's told, hocking a dark wad of saliva into the dirt.

"See. Water ain't black."

The boy spits again, and it's still black. He wipes some sand off the apple, and takes a big, juicy bite. He swallows, then spits again. Now it's gray.

"Almost alive again!" the boy says, proudly. "My daddy once said an apple is just as good as a canteen. He said you can drink anything if you have to. Even a horse."

The boy takes another big bite, swallows hard, then spits right at the Ranger's boots. The boy's saliva is as clear as raindrops now, and he smiles and holds out the apple to the Ranger.

"Wanna bite?"

"No, thanks. Too late for that. My mouth may be cracked, but it don't hurt. Cuts only start hurting if you put water on them. People, too."

The boy laughs around another chunk of apple.

"So you're saying you don't eat apples or drink water? And you did this for a year?"

"I don't know what they teach you in school, but water is not what's pumping through our hearts."

The boy raises an eyebrow, then, holding the apple core in his mouth, he runs the sharp tip of the rock along a vein in his small arm thoughtfully.

"Buncha windies," he says.

"Watch it, kid. If anything's pointy enough to cut your apple, it's pointy enough to cut you. That's what the Sioux used to say. Never run with a sharp rock."

Taking it as a challenge, the boy runs, worried this confused old man will change his mind again and take back the gift.

"Are you listening to me, kid? Be careful with that trigger! It'll blow that tiny hand of yours right the hell off!"

The boy turns and run backwards, looking at the Ranger, then back down at his rock. His grin is lupine and familiar.

"No, it won't. It only did that because our daddy told it to."

TWENTY
EIGHT

A Gun Named Sioux

"The tears are welling in my eyes again,
I need twenty big buckets to catch them in.
Twenty pretty girls to carry them down,
Twenty deep holes to bury them in."
-Nick Cave, "Hallelujah"

Agua Fría. Day before tomorrow.

A young man with a wild tangle of orange curls is standing at a well, morning fog swirling around his boots. He cranks the handle and lowers the bucket. He watches the rope unroll, watches the bucket disappear into the dark, watches the handle turn and turn and turn until it disappears. The rope never ends, and the bucket never hits bottom. He spins the handle faster, as fast as his arm will allow. Sweat runs off his nose, and the rope continues to snake into the dark. He cranks the handle until his hand slips and he falls to the ground. He looks up and sees the same coil of rope he started with. Scowling, he hitches his belt tight and comes up with a rusted, busted weapon. He throws it in the well after the bucket and never hears it hit bottom either.

Panic settling in his gut, he contemplates throwing everyone in the world into the well, just to prove it ends, just to prove he's not crazy. He reaches for the handle again, and with one mighty crank sends it spinning freely without the strain of his shoulders.

After what seems like hours, there's finally the echo of a thud as the bucket hits something solid. He gives it a couple spins in the other direction, then lets the bucket drop again.

This time there's a splash.

As he hauls the bucket back up, he pauses to wave to his mother in the distance, leading a calf across the prairie.

After a moment, he's finally secured one bucket of water, at the price of his sanity, and he heads back for home. At some point, he stops to steady the bucket from rocking and spilling its treasure, and notices a boy on a horse in the distance. It's hot, but besides his strip of breechcloth, this boy also has a buffalo skin draped over his bare shoulders. And this boy is young, but still wears a headband of beads and feathers. He's walking his horse around a wooden sign in the ground that reads:

Agua Fria - Population - 2

He puts a small hand over the splintered words, and after a couple kicks and whinnies, he's rocked the sign post loose from the soil. His animal walks over it like it was never there.

There's a flash of light as a sunbeam shines through a hole in the horse's head.

After a few more steps, the native boy's horse is running, the feather on his head flapping. A few more steps after that, the feather slips free from its headband, and the horse's feet no longer touch the ground.

The young man with the red hair keeps walking. When he's home, he realizes his bucket is empty, that it was always empty.

***

Desert. Same day.

The skeleton of a dog lies in the middle of a half-moon dune, its bones picked clean, a glimmer of a copper penny in its ribcage. Ribbons of shredded black clothing weave through the vertebrae, and lying near the grinning skull are three revolvers, dull from exposure, sand filling their barrels and covering their triggers. The hammer of one pistol is cocked.

EPILOGUE

The Last Hole

"Tell that long-tongued liar, tell that midnight rider,
the rambler, the gambler, the back-biter,
sooner or later, God's gonna cut you down."
-Johnny Cash, "God's Gonna Cut You Down"

Bisbée. Some time in the future, but soon.

The Ranger strides through a field once overgrown with weeds, long since baked brown by the sun. He walks tall but slow, crunching and snapping through the decay, stopping when he comes to a black, rusted horseshoe barely visible in the dirt. His tongue starts working around his teeth like he's fixing to talk, but the sound of his own voice is a distant memory, a forgotten riddle. He kicks the lifeless dirt around the horseshoe to reveal a small doorway into the earth.

This used to be a well, Bob's father told him once. *But they filled it in, long ago, back when your sister was getting married, before she had to move away in disgrace, before her belly started to show.*

"It will be March," the Ranger mutters, trying to recite his father's calendar, but hearing Samuel's voice instead of his own.

"'March is the first month warm enough to sit on the ground. But October is the first month cold enough to sleep under the ground...'"

The Ranger tries humming a folk song his dad hated so that he'll stop doing all the talking.

"*Hmm-hmm hmmm hmmm hmmm... o' jury, would you call me a liar... I never killed that man, never started that fire... he was a bad man, o' cruel Stack O' Lee... they give him the road...*"

The Ranger crouches down, flinches as his old joints crack

like twigs, then he pulls up on the horseshoe with the last of his strength to open a door leading to nothing. But the tornado shelter isn't filled in like he left it, even though his uncle made him swing most of those shovelfuls himself. The hole is deep, like it was just dug.

"All my eye," the Ranger says, incredulous.

Then without hesitation, without a glance at the sky, without looking around, down, or behind, he climbs a ladder deep into the hole and disappears into the dark.

The door slams shut behind him, and a green snake slips in and out of the horseshoe, chasing its tail faster and faster, desperate to follow the dead.

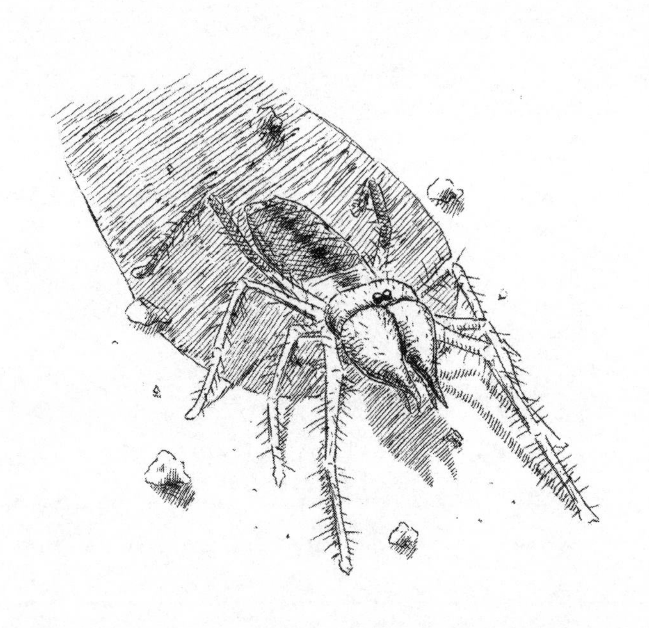

"Times like these, we have to start using words a little different..."
-Toothless

Glossary

noun 1. Saloon or bar where hyperbole and exaggeration is encouraged. 2. Confessional booth where people routinely "gloss" over responsibility and/or transgressions. 3. Shoe-shine box.

Acorn – *noun* 1. Runt or weakling, usually refers to livestock. 2. Term of endearment.

Adam's Ale – *noun* 1. Water. 2. Snake venom. 3. One's own urine.

Addle-headed – *adjective* 1. Dumb, confused. 2. Forgetful. 3. Nodding in recognition.

Ain't – *contraction* 1. Am not, are not, is not. 2. When something is not what it should be.

Airish – *adjective* 1. Chilly, breezy. 2. Deceptively silent or still. 3. Irish homeless/vagrant.

All My Eye – *exclamation* 1. Ridiculous, impossible. 2. Goodbye.

Among the Willows – *idiom* 1. On the run, lawless. 2. Hiding among willow trees.

Angelica – *noun* Young woman, not spoken for.

Animus Revertendi – *Latin* "With intention to return"; *idiom* "With intention to eat."

Apple – *noun* 1. Round tree fruit of the rose family, typically with red or green skin. 2. Saddle horn. 3. Head of the penis. 4. Pomegranate. *biblical*

Apple Jack – *noun* 1. Hard cider or brandy. 2. Man who sexually penetrates pomegranates.

Apple Peeler – *noun* 1. Pocketknife. 2. Masturbation hand.

Argufy – *verb* 1. To argue. 2. To argue in an effeminate tone.

Atween – *preposition* Between things that are "atwixt."

Atwixt – *preposition* Between.

Auger – *noun* 1. Hole-boring tool. 2. Boss, leader.

Bad Box – *noun* 1. Dangerous situation or predicament. 2. Diseased female.

Bad Egg – *noun* 1. Untrustworthy or disreputable person. 2. Diseased male.

Bad Medicine – *noun* 1. Bad news 2. Spoiled whiskey.

Bag of Nails - *idiom* Out of control, hectic, confusing; *noun* Hat full of burrs or thorns.

Ballast – *noun* 1. Money. 2. Women. 3. Wealthy women.

Bangtail – *noun* 1. Wild, unbroken horse. 2. Mustang 3. Armed prostitute.

Barking Iron – *noun* Pistol.

Barking Spider – *noun* 1. Someone firing multiple pistols simultaneously. 2. Flatulence.

Bay – *noun* 1. Light-colored horse, usually red. 2. Old woman.

Bean-eater – *noun* 1. Mexican 2. Someone who enjoys cunnilingus.

Beat the Dutch – *idiom* 1. To surpass expectations or "beat the devil." 2. To win against great odds.

Bed Down – *verb* 1. To murder. 2. To fornicate 3. To fornicate with a corpse.

Beef-headed – *adjective* 1. Dumb, dull. 2. Sunburned.

Beeline – *noun* 1. Direct path between two places 2. The random, erratic path a bee travels between its colony and pollination due to genetic anomaly or mutation.

Been in the Sun – *idiom* 1. Drunk. 2. Post-coital glow.

Bend an Elbow – *verb* 1. To drink. 2. To masturbate with your gun hand.

B'hoy – *noun* Rowdy, young male, ruffian.

Big Fifty – *noun* Long .50-caliber Sharps rifle popularized by buffalo hunters.

Biggity – *adjective* 1. Large, impressive, haughty. 2. Swollen, engorged.

Biscuit – *noun* 1. Saddle horn. 2. Egg.

Biscuit Eater – *noun* 1. Egg-stealing dog. 2. Egg-stealing man.

Biscuit Man – *noun* Egg-stealing-dog stealing man.

Bite the Ground – *idiom* 1. To be shot dead. 2. To pretend to be shot dead, play possum.

Blame – *adjective* Used in place of "damn" for emphasis to express frustration or surprise.

Blarney – *noun* Tall tales, idle discourse.

Blue – *adjective* 1. Drunk 2. Sad 3. Asphyxiated.

Blusteration – *noun* 1. Ramblings of a drunkard, braggart. 2. Unexpected prairie wind. 3. Flatulence.

Bobbed – *adjective* 1. Clipped, shorn. 2. Alert.

Box Herder – *noun* Person in charge of managing prostitutes at a brothel.

Breech Cloth – *noun* Leather, cloth or bark-bast (fiber from the bark of linden or birch trees) worn by Native Americans to cover genitals.

Bub – *noun* 1. Brother. 2. Short for "bubble," specifically mucus or semen.

Buckle Bunnies *noun* 1. Female fans of cowboys and rodeo stars. 2. Homosexuals.

Bugle on the Bowl *idiom* Harmonic flatulence while seated on a toilet.

Bushwhack – *verb* 1. To ambush, surprise. 2. To masturbate outdoors.

Buster – *noun* 1. Large, powerful man. 2. Anything big or impressive.

Calico – *noun* 1. Flashy female, prostitute. 2. A "paint" horse, Native American ponies with irregular white patches on its skin. 3. Cat meat.

California Collar – *noun* Hangman's noose.

Catbirds and Bushtits – *idiom* Nothing.

Cavallard – *noun* 1. Caravan. 2. Cavalry. 3. Cavalcade. 4. Caveators. 5. Invisible friends.

Caveson – *noun* 1. Muzzle or mouth. 2. Mouth with bad breath.

Celestial – *noun* People of Chinese descent, a reference to the "Celestial Empire."

Chickabiddy – *noun* 1. Baby chicken. 2. Term of endearment.

Choke the Horn – *idiom* To grab the saddle horn on a bucking horse (derogatory); *verb* Masturbate

Clear Leather – *verb* 1. To pull a weapon from the holster 2. To draw quickly draw during a gunfight.

Coffin Varnish – *noun* 1. Whiskey, wine. 2. Coffin varnish.

Converter – *noun* 1. Preacher. 2. An unpersuasive person.

Corned – *adjective* 1. Drunk. 2. Recently sodomized.

Cottonwood Blossom – *noun* A recently-lynched corpse hanging from a tree limb.

Crack – *adjective* 1. The best, most skilled. 2. Unholy.

Cracker – *noun* 1. White, rural, poor person, derived from the whip "cracking" of slave-owners. 2. Someone who believes conjecture they secretly find flattering or appealing.

Crowbait – *adjective* Slow or unreliable, usually refers to a horse; *noun* Filthy or unclean saddle.

Cunne – *Latin* 1. Cunt. 2. Someone else's mother. 3. Someone else's grandmother. 4. Someone else's daughter.

Custard – *noun* Semen.

Dang – *exclamation* Euphemism for "Damn"; *adjective* Short for "Dangerous."

Dogged – *adjective* Tired, ragged.

Doxology Works – *noun* 1. Church. 2. Bar or saloon constructed from an old church.

Dry-gulch – *verb* 1. To sucker punch. 2. To ambush from a ditch or gulch.

Dusted – *adjective* 1. Thrown from a horse. 2. Covered in dust. 3. Covered in dry feces.

Dutch – *noun* Devil.

Eggbound – *adjective* 1. Medical condition in birds or reptiles where the female is unable to pass a fully-formed egg, usually refers to chickens. 2. Frozen by indecision or fear.

Eggsucker – *noun* 1. Person with an unbreakable habit, including but not limited to egg-sucking 2. Thief or untrustworthy person. 3. Excessive flatterer or sycophant.

Exoduster – *noun* 1. Dirt-covered settlers 2. African-American emigrants or freed slaves who departed the post-Civil War South in search of work.

Farging – *exclamation* Euphemism for "fucking."

Ferae Naturae – *Latin phrase* "Wild beast"; *idiom* "Fair game."

Fish – *noun* Cowboy's rain slicker manufactured by the East Coast Pommel Co., whose logo depicted a fish. They required oiling and waxing and were very flammable around campfires.

Frog – *noun* 1. Child. 2. Runt.

Fox – *verb* To fix, usually refers to fixing boots by adding new soles.

G'hal – *noun* Rowdy, young female, reveler.

Gig – *verb* 1. To vigorously spur a horse. 2. To sodomize.

Go See the Elephant – *euphemism* 1. Go to town. 2. Go to court.

Gone Coon – *noun* 1. Dead man. 2. Dying man, past recovery.

Granger – *noun* 1. Farmer (derogatory). 2. Lawman (complimentary).

Groggery – *noun* 1. Bar or saloon. 2. Church constructed from a former bar or saloon.

Guttersnipe – *noun* Homeless child, orphan; *verb* To shoot homeless children or orphans with a long rifle from a distance.

Hangdog – *adjective* Dejected or guilty appearance, shame-faced; *noun* Dog used to test the strength of a hangman's rope.

Harp – *noun* Harmonica; *verb* To harass, pester.

Hawk – *verb* Hock, hack, or spit with enough velocity for a bird to snatch.

Hearn – *verb* To hear

Heeled – *adjective* 1. Wearing shoes 2. Armed.

Hemp – *noun* 1. Rope. 2. Noose.

High-binder – *noun* 1. Dangerous or disreputable man. 2. Strong and respectable horse.

Honey Bucket – *noun* 1. Bucket used for excrement. 2. Bucket used to carry any foul substance.

Honey-fuggle – *verb* To cheat, defraud.

Hoss – *noun* 1. Horse. 2. Person or small animal disguised as a horse.

H'penny Dreadfuller – *noun* Variant of "Penny Dreadful," 19th century British publications featuring lurid content printed on cheap wood pulp.

Hurricane Deck – *noun* 1. Saddle on a bucking bronco. 2. Card-flinging tantrum thrown by a losing poker dealer.

Illy – *adjective* 1. Sick. 2. Dizzying, impressive.

Jackeroo – *noun* 1. Young cowboy. 2. Buckaroo who's been caught masturbating.

Jerk Steak – *noun* 1. Fly-ridden beef jerky. 2. Penis stretched from frantic, excessive masturbation.

Joy Juice – *noun* 1. Whiskey. 2. Semen.

Judas Steer – *noun* 1. Male bovine that leads other cattle to slaughter. Typically spared the hook and used repeatedly. 2. Male bovine that leads other cattle to slaughter, only to be killed first.

Keep It Dry – *idiom* 1. Maintain secrecy. 2. Endorse the withdraw method of birth control.

Kenosis – *noun* Jesus Christ's rejection of divinity after embracing his human form.

Knock Galley West – *verb* To pummel or beat senseless; *noun* A pummeling or severe beating.

Lacing – *noun* A one-sided beating.

Laddy – *noun* 1. Young boy, variant of "laddie." 2. Young girl, variant of "lassie."

Lambast – *verb* To viciously beat or deride.

Latchpan – *noun* 1. Lower lip. 2. Scrotum.

Lathy – *adjective* 1. Slender, skeletal. 2. Covered with thin, flat laths of wood.

Leafless Tree – *noun* 1. Gallows. 2. Small-breasted woman.

Lickfinger – *noun* 1. Person who shows obsequiousness or eagerness to please. 2. Politician.

Limsy – *adjective* 1. Weak, loose, flexible, variant of "flimsy." 2. Drunk.

Loco – *adjective* 1. Confused, foolish, Spanish for "crazy." 2. Reasonable.

Loopy – *adjective* 1. Confused, foolish. 2. Drunk.

Lubber – *noun* 1. Large, sturdy male. 2. Short for "landlubber." 3. Clumsy person.

Mamacita – *noun* Mother, diminutive form of "mamá," Spanish for "mum."

Marble – *noun* Eyeball; *verb* To leave or move away.

May Hay – *verb* To cause confusion, put in disorder; *noun* Someone who performs sex acts in a hay pile or on a hay bale.

Mayhap – *adverb* Perhaps, possibly.

Miss Nancy – *noun* 1. Effeminate male. 2. Unmarried effeminate male.

Mockered – *adjective* 1. Dirty, defiled. 2. Drunk.

Molly – *noun* 1. Effeminate male. 2. Engaged effeminate male.

Moppy – *adjective* 1. Drunk, tipsy. 2. Punchy, excitable.

Mousing – *verb* 1. To sneak around undetected. 2. To steal food. 3. To hunt or catch mice.

Mud Pipes – *noun* 1. Riding boots. 2. Pants filled with excrement.

Mugwump – *noun* 1. Algonquian term for "war leader," kingpin 2. Someone with political independence. 3. Seductive, demure creature. 4. Addict.

Music Roots – *noun* 1. Sweet potatoes. 2. Overripe vegetable.

Mutton-puncher – *noun* Cowboy or herder who sodomizes sheep.

Nail to the Counter – *verb* 1. To catch someone in a lie, prove deception. 2. To sodomize.

Nibbler – *noun* 1. Petty thief. 2. Variant of "nipper."

Nipper – *noun* 1. Infant or small child. 2. Teething child. 3. Forceps or gripping tool. 4. Dentures.

Nit – *noun* 1. Egg or larvae of a head louse. 2. Foolish person, short for "nitwit."

Nobby – *adjective* 1. Expensive, stylish. 2. Well-endowed.

Nose Paint – *noun* 1. High-grain alcohol. 2. Horse bridle.

On the Lamb – *idiom* On the run, lawless; *verb* To sexually penetrate sheep or livestock.

On the Prod – *idiom* 1. Person or persons looking for trouble, a criminal on the prowl. 2. An enraged animal.

Owl Hoot – *noun* 1. Outlaw. 2. Seamstress.

Oxbows – *noun* Large, wooden stirrups, also known as "oxyokes."

Painting One's Tonsils – *verb* To drink alcohol, variant of "painting one's nose."

Pancake – *noun* 1. Small English saddle (derogatory). 2. Cow chip, excrement.

Pig Iron – *noun* 1. Crude, substandard iron leftover during the smelting process. 2. Mixed alloy.

Plaguily – *adverb* 1. Exceedingly, dreadfully. 2. Extraordinarily.

Prospected – *adjective* 1. Investigated for the possibility of profit. 2. Stolen; *verb* To court a woman.

Pull Foot – *verb* 1. To flee, leave in a hurry. 2. To masturbate.

Pulling in the Pieces – *verb* 1. To make money. 2. To steal money.

Pung – *noun* A makeshift sleigh constructed of boards and boxes, pulled by a horse.

Quirley – *noun* Pig's tail; *verb* To roll a cigarette.

Quirt – *noun* 1. Short stock whip, typically with two tassels. 2. White, rural poor person.

'Ranger – *noun* 1. Ape, variant of "orangutan." 2. Red-haired child.

Reckon – *verb* To guess or offer conjecture; *noun* Comeuppance, variant of "reckoning."

Roastineers – *noun* 1. Corn roasted inside the husk. 2. Person who gossips libelously; *verb* To gossip libelously, derived from to "roast an ear."

Ruckus – *noun* Noisy disturbance, a fight; *verb* To commit a small transgression that leads to a larger incident.

Rum Hole – *noun* 1. Small saloon or bar. 2. Mouth. 3. Diarrhea-ridden anus.

Rusher – *noun* 1. Important person, flashy politician or clergyman. 2. Someone who brings a knife to a gunfight, not caring that it's a gunfight.

Sand – *noun* 1. Courage, fortitude. 2. Large or swollen scrotum. 3. Mumps.

Saphead – *noun* 1. Idiot, fool. 2. Someone who drools. 3. Someone who miraculously survives a gaping head wound.

Scrub – *noun* 1. A small horse of little value. 2. Someone unable to find love amongst their own species. 3. Someone who hangs their head from the window of an acquaintance's carriage, hollering or whistling at females.

Shanny – *noun* 1. Jester or clown, foolish but adept on his/her feet. 2. Someone who resembles a coyote or dog. 3. The offspring of someone who resembles a coyote or dog.

Shave Tail – *noun* 1. Greenhorn, novice. 2. Flap of skin on the cheek or chin due to inexperience shaving. 3. Someone with a flap of skin on the cheek or chin due to inexperience shaving.

Shitfire – *exclamation* Damn, dang; *noun* Flatulence.

Shoal – *verb* 1. To lounge about lazily. 2. To wander aimlessly. 3. To scalp a corpse.

Shut Your Cock Holster – *idiom* Shut your mouth; *verb* 1. To fix a chicken coop. 2. To nest.

Skin – *verb* 1. To put a hand on the handle of a weapon. 2. To draw a weapon from its holster; *noun* An overly vigorous, scarring hand job.

Slayed – *verb* To surprise, cheat; *noun* Abuse, quarrel, variant of "slate."

Slogging – *noun* 1. A beating, thrashing. 2. Frustratingly evenly-matched fight, long scuffle.

Smelt – *noun* A small, freshwater fish of the Osmeridae family, common to the North American Great Lakes; *verb* To extract metal from iron ore by fire.

Snake Oil Salesman – *noun* 1. Someone who knowingly sells fraudulent goods. 2. Someone who sells you exactly what you need at that moment.

Squaw Wood – *noun* 1. Smaller dead branches or limbs under a tree's live canopy, named for the easy a female tribeswoman would gather wood without an axe. 2. Penis. 3. Cow chips, excrement.

Squeeze the Biscuit – *verb* 1. To grab the saddle horn on a bucking horse (derogatory). 2. To masturbate. 3. To choke the horn.

Squirrel – *verb* To hide; *noun* Someone who feeds squirrels though they are starving.

Stew – *verb* To sulk, pout; *noun* 1. Confusion of mind, funk. 2. A male Sioux.

Sucker – *noun* 1. Hard candy on a stick. 2. A nursing newborn.

Sue – *noun* Any Sioux tribesman or tribeswoman.

Take the Big Jump – *verb* 1. To die. 2. To fly.

Tangle-footed – *adjective* 1. Drunk, stumbling. 2. Drunk from cheap or low-quality whiskey.

Taradiddies – *noun* 1. Half-truth, parable. 2. Diarrhea. 3. Song sung in four parts. 4. Any passionless coupling.

Tendsome – *adjective* Fussy or unruly child; *verb* To ask questions that you already know the answer to.

Time to Paddle – *idiom* Time to leave, flee; *noun* The amount of time between the current time and an impending beating.

Tiswin – *noun* 1. Someone you hate for no good reason. 2. Weak Apache beer, brewed from corn.

Tongue Oil – *noun* 1. Alcohol, specifically whiskey. 2. Maple syrup. 3. Any liquid to remedy dry mouth or coughing.

Tongue-foot – *noun* A stupid person, prone to mouth-breathing.

Train Bible – *noun* 1. Deck of playing cards. 2. Cheap paperback novel used as a diary by vagrants, typically detailing sexual conquests and/or money-saving recipes.

Trio – *noun* 1. Three foolish people. 2. Tree with a hangman's noose dangling from a lower branch, derivative of "Tree-O." 3. A tree supporting a child's swing constructed from a wagon wheel.

Trounce – *noun* 1. Beating. 2. Affectionate tackle.

True Blue – *adjective* 1. Courageous. 2. Deceptive; *noun* Someone who pretends to be allied with the Confederacy or the South, but is in reality a Union sympathizer.

Tub-thumper – *noun* 1. Tent or street preacher. 2. A wandering preacher or religious man in need of a church or congregation.

Undertook – *verb* 1. To take upon oneself a task or performance, to attempt. 2. To promise or obligate oneself. 3. To take charge of, assume a duty; *adjective* Recently deceased, in need of an undertaker.

Varmit – *noun* 1. Small mammal, variant of "varmint." 2. Vermin. 3. Someone with no religious beliefs, infidel, heathen, nonbeliever. 4. Nonbeliever who is proven correct on his/her deathbed.

Vocō – *Latin* 1. "Invoke, declare." 2. "I forget."

Wabble – *verb* 1. To sway or swerve dangerously, variant of "wobble." 2. To babble incoherently while sober. 3. To move one's mouth in anticipation of responding while someone else is speaking. 4. To dance without music while inebriated. 5. To do anything.

Wakin' Snakes – *verb* 1. To raise a ruckus, cause problems. 2. To drink alcohol and sing out of tune.

Whaler – *noun* 1. Strapping man or woman. 2. Whaling ship. 3. Large seaman. 4. Large volume of semen.

Windies – *noun* 1. Complete falsehood, lie. 2. Deception disguised as a "taradiddy." 3. Flatulence.

Wipe Your Chin – *idiom* 1. Be quiet. 2. Stop staring. 3. Be wary of insects on your face.

Worm Fence – *noun* 1. Collapsing, decrepit fence. 2. Rail fence laid in a zig-zag manner. 3. Awkward sexual situation.

Wreckin' – *verb* 1. To guess or offer conjecture in a destructive manner, variant of "reckon."

Xanthie – *noun* 1. Short for "Xanthippe," the wife of Socrates. 2. Ill-tempered woman, harpy.

Yaff – *verb* To bark; *noun* Flatulence.

Yean – *verb* To give birth, specifically to a lamb; *noun* Breech birth.

Yellows – *noun* Disease affecting horse or cattle, indicated by a yellowing of the eyes; *adjective* Cowardice, fearfulness, variant of "cheese-livered."

Zapata – *noun* Wide "Mexican" moustache, named after Emiliano Zapata Salazar.

Zig-zag – *noun* Sex; *verb* 1. To have sex. 2. To unsuccessfully attempt sex.

Zoon – *verb* 1. To bark, chatter, chirp, croak, grunt, hiss, hum, screech, roar, snarl, trill, yelp. 2. To cry, typically at the sky, while armed.

"Because Cowboy Dan's a major player in the cowboy scene,
He goes to the reservation, drinks and gets mean.
He goes the desert, fires his rifle in the sky,
And says, 'God if I have to die, you will have to die.'
-Modest Mouse, "Cowboy Dan"

Acknowledgements

Besides my dad, I would like to thank my favorite westerns, or any movie that deep down inside wanted to be a western, but especially westerns with spaghetti sauce all over 'em, including *Per Un Pugno Di Dollari* (a.k.a. *A Fistful of Dollars), Per Qualche Dollaro In Più* (a.k.a. *For a Few Dollars More), Il Buono, il Brutto, il Cattivo,* (a.k.a. *The Good, the Bad, and the Ugly), Giù la Testa,* (a.k.a. *A Fistful of Dynamite,* a.k.a. *Duck, You Sucker,* a.k.a. *Once Upon A Time: The Revolution), McCabe & Mrs. Miller, Yojimbo, Last Man Standing, The Quick and the Dead, Unforgiven, Dead Man, The Assassination of Jesse James by the Coward Robert Ford, Deadwood, Ride the High Country, The Wild Bunch, The Ballad of Cable Hogue, Pat Garrett and Billy the Kid, Appaloosa, Bring Me the Head of Alfredo Garcia, The Mission, Tombstone, Utu, Undead,* (or anything else with a four-barreled shotgun), *The Outlaw Jose Wales, Duel in the Sun, Major Dundee, Ravenous* (now that's how you introduce a hero), *Django, Django, Kill! (If You Live, Shoot!)* (a.k.a. *Oro Hondo,* a.k.a. *Se Sei Vivo, Spara), Django Unchained,* most of the *Djangos* really, *The Way of the Gun, Westworld, Wild Bill, The Proposition, Lawless* (and anything else Nick Cave writes in the future), *Heaven's Gate,* half the *Zulu* movies, *Extreme Prejudice, C'era uno Volta il West,* (a.k.a. *Once Upon A Time In The West), C'era uno Volta il Amerigo* (a.k.a.

Once Upon A Time In America), Once Upon a Time in Mexico (a.k.a. *Everybody Hates That Movie*, but fuck it, he shoots the cook, and you need a trilogy to restore balance*), Le Dernier Combat* (a.k.a. The *Last Battle), The Searchers, Kung Fu Hustle* (a.k.a. *King Fusion*, such a western), *I Quattro dell'apocalisse* (a.k.a. *Four of the Apocalypse), Geronimo, Open Range* (for the candy-bar scene alone), *Six-String Samurai, Giant, High Noon, Outland, The Three Burials of Melquiades Estrada, Jonah Hex, Black Robe, The Long Riders, Mannaja* (a.k.a. *A Man Called Blade), El Mariachi, Desperado, The Rundown, One Eyed Jacks, Pale Rider, Run Man Run* (a.k.a. *Corri uomo corri*, a.k.a. *Big Gundown 2), Sukiyaki Western Django, 3:10 to Yuma* (both versions), *Junior Bonner, True Grit* (both versions), *Quigley Down Under* (not both versions, just the one with Magnum P.I.), and all three *Young Guns* films (I'm being optimistic). And thanks to my trivia team, Senile Felines, for helping to come up with all them extra cowboy words. And Marty Robbins, of course, for that song. Do I have to even say it? Thanks, Team Pig Iron, for all the hard work on the book: Jason Stuart, Mark Rapacz, Tony McMillen, Dyer Wilk, Sean Leonard and Amy Lueck. And thanks to Jedidiah Ayres, Scott Phillips, and especially the late, great Cortright McMeel for the night of the "acid western brainstorm" at that bar in St. Louis that also inspired this thing.

About the Author

David James Keaton's award-winning fiction has appeared in over 50 publications, including *The Big Adios*, *Grift*, *Beat to a Pulp*, *Noir at the Bar II*, and *Pulp Modern*. His first collection, *Fish Bites Cop! Stories to Bash Authorities* (Comet Press), was named the 2014 This Is Horror Short Story Collection of the Year and was a finalist for the Killer Nashville Silver Falchion Award. His first novel, *The Last Projector* (Broken River Books), was released in 2014. He lives in Kentucky with his wife, a furlong of western films, and an overflowing stable of senile felines.

This novel was loosely inspired by the song...

PIG IRON

words and music by Arty Stealins

To the town of Agua Fria rode some strangers one hot day
A man who hated horses to avenge a friend named Gray
The other stranger was a smartass prone to sarcastic quips
Who knew the Ranger would be doomed with that pig iron on his hip
Pig iron on his hip

It was early in the morning when they proceeded into town
Where water had grown scarce and fires raging all around
"Who the hell hates horses?" came the whisper from each lip
And can a man even fire from a pig iron on his hip?
Pig iron on his hip

In this town there lived a psycho by the name of Texas Red
Befriended by dead dogs in a well, all were left for dead
He was vicious and confusing and rode a horse that wouldn't die
Though he'd taken his own pistol and shot it in the eye
Shot it in the eye

One of the strangers started talking made it plain to all their ears
He was an Arizona ranger in the twilight of his years
He'd come to get his sister, after killing Texas Red
Always thought his shelf might look nice with that motherfucker's head
Motherfucker's head

Wasn't long before the story found its way to Red's young gang
They killed the Ranger's final friend, vowed to see the Ranger hang
But weren't as worried about the Ranger as they'd seen him make the slip
Carried a gun made of pig iron that exploded on his hip
Exploded on his hip

The morning passed so quickly that everybody beat their feet
No doubt it was around noon time when they walked out in the street
Heads hung heavy and they swore the Ranger would be mourned
But a boy had found Red's holster and filled it full of thorns
Filled it full of thorns.

It was fifty feet between them but who could really say
And the swiftness of that fire is still talked about today
Red had not cleared leather as those thorns held him fast
And a Ranger's middle finger pointing was the thing that he saw last
Thing that he saw last

Not a single shot was fired and the folks all gathered round
The burning body of the outlaw laid out upon the ground
He may have gone on being crazy but he made one fatal slip
When he fought a man who hated horses and the pig iron on his hip
Pig iron on his hip

Made in the USA
Middletown, DE
25 August 2015